THE PLACE OF REFUGE

the Place of Refuge

a novella

Albert Tucher

SHOTGUN HONEY

Published by Shotgun Honey, an imprint of Down & Out Books

Shotgun Honey
PO Box 75272
Charleston, WV 25375
www.ShotgunHoney.com

Down & Out Books
3959 Van Dyke Rd, Ste. 265
Lutz, FL 33558
www.DownAndOutBooks.com

Cover Design by Bad Fido.

First Printing 2017

ISBN-10: 1-943402-61-2
ISBN-13: 978-1-943402-61-8

In loving memory of
Albert Tucher (1926-2011) and
Doris Tucher (1925-2012)

The Place of Refuge

FEBRUARY

1

"NOW THAT," COUTINHO SAID, "is not what the Chamber of Commerce wants to see."

As soon as said the words, he wanted them back. It wasn't his style to get flippant over a body.

He had seen death before. Even in paradise people had fatal accidents. Bar fights could end as badly in Hilo as anywhere else, and Hawaii had its share of unfortunates with no one but the police to find them in the end.

But this kind of butchery was something new. Even in Honolulu the cops didn't see much of it, and the Big Island wasn't the big city.

His partner circled the body at a distance to get a look at the woman's face.

"Gladys Robles," said Kim. "Can't say she deserved to go like this."

"Who does?"

Coutinho found the odors of death, of blood and bowels,

more oppressive than usual. A glance told him that Kim felt the same.

Here was the vulnerability of prostitutes, spelled out in smears of blood on the wall and puddles of it on the floor. The body's position suggested that Gladys had slid down the wall as she lost consciousness. There were some distinct handprints among the streaks of blood, but they were probably hers.

If they were lucky, some of the blood would be the moke's. He might have cut himself in his killing frenzy.

Coutinho didn't feel lucky.

The crime scene techs obviously wanted the detectives out of the way. Coutinho turned and left the hotel room with Kim behind him. In the hallway the Filipino housekeeper who had found the body leaned against the wall as if grateful for its support. She was new enough on the island to be wondering whether this kind of thing came with her job.

"Did you see the young lady arrive?"

"Yes, I see her. She give me forty dollars."

To clean up after the day's work and keep an eye on things as much as she could.

"How about her gentlemen callers?"

"I see a couple of them. I have my work to do."

"So you didn't see the last one?"

"No, Sir."

If she had, Coutinho might be working a double murder.

"Thanks. You can go back to work."

Or back home to Manila, if her nerve failed her. He wouldn't blame her if it did.

He would have to talk to the desk clerk and the maintenance workers, but he expected similar answers from them.

Right now he decided to get a breath of air. Outside it was misting a little, but real rain had been scarce for months.

From the sidewalk in front of the hotel he could see a piece of Hilo Bay, with the usual dark clouds on the horizon. They seemed to warn coastal dwellers to head for higher ground.

Coutinho lifted the hem of his aloha shirt and took his cell phone from his belt. Lieutenant Tanaka answered the second ring.

"How bad?" said Tanaka.

"I hope they don't come much worse."

"Anything to work with?"

"Doesn't look like he cooperated by dropping his driver's license or anything."

"So if the techs get no fingerprints or DNA, we'll have to wait for the moke to do it again."

2

JESSIE LOOKED AT TEDDY DIAS and thought about having his children.

What got her thinking that way was the look of fatherly indulgence on his face, which was a little weird, considering. Teddy was watching two of his underlings administer a beat-down to a surfer-dealer named Vince, who had come up short on his money.

Vince wasn't enjoying himself, but he seemed to realize that it could be worse. The two men using their fists on him worked without noticeable enthusiasm. The crowd in Lori's Bar stayed true to the North Shore surfer's code of conduct and went about their drinking and palavering as if they saw nothing. And Jessie found herself ignoring the spectacle in favor of June Cleaver fantasies of life with Teddy.

It was more than a little weird.

"Okay," said Teddy. "Gabe, Frank, that's enough."

Gabe was holding Vince up while Frank gave the surfer's

ribs some extra attention. Frank let fly with one more gut punch.

"Frank," said Teddy, "that was unnecessary."

The false benevolence was supposed to make Vince feel grateful to the same man who had ordered his pain. Teddy knew it, Vince knew it, and Jessie understood it too. She could tell that Frank didn't take the rebuke seriously.

Gabe let Vince fall to the floor, which was probably the worst part of his punishment. Six different kinds of tetanus lurked down there.

Teddy reached his arm around Jessie's shoulders. She recalled the first time he had done that. She had wanted to cringe, but at some point that urge had faded. She could feel the thrum of blood under his skin. He would be hot for her tonight, and she wouldn't have a problem with that.

Across the table, Teddy's new friend Chuey put a sycophantic grin on his face.

"Hey, Teddy, you run a tight operation. My uncle's gonna like that."

Jessie didn't like the young man, but she didn't expect her opinion to count.

Teddy stroked her hair.

"So," he said, "how'd you like to go to Mexico."

"As long as it's with you, Teddy."

He turned back toward Chuey and grinned.

"The boss here says we're good to go. Let's talk details."

From the beginning Jessie had pretended that details bored her. She still had trouble believing that Teddy bought her airhead act, but here was this up-and-coming *pakalolo* dealer talking shop right in front of her.

She listened for a while, but not long enough to make him wonder. Then she turned to Delilah.

"Am I going to like Nogales?"

Chuey's girlfriend smiled back.

"Home is where the heart is. I like it because Chuey's there."

"You ever feel homesick?"

"A little, but not for here. For Vegas. That's where I met Chuey."

"How long you been in Vegas?"

"Couple of years."

Jessie knew that story. Economic refugees from Hawaii made a major contribution toward keeping the Vegas casinos and hotels going. At some point, someone from Hawaii must have caught on in Nevada and told his cousins and his cousins' friends, and now there was a revolving door.

"What brings you back here?" said Jessie.

"*Ohana.*"

Family. The word explained a lot in Hawaii.

"Chuey wants to meet them. Seriously, though, you'll like Mexico. There's even a few of us there."

"No kidding."

"One guy I'm thinking of in particular. King Kamehameha come back to life."

"What's his name?"

"Hosea," said Delilah.

Jessie didn't realize at first that she was staring, but then she noticed the strange look that Delilah was giving her.

"Hosea what?"

"Huh," said Delilah after a moment. "I don't think I ever heard his last name. He's just Hosea. That's kind of the way it goes there. Lots of people are vague about who they are, or how they got there. Especially how they got there."

Jessie got up from her seat.

"Going to the ladies'?"

Delilah didn't get up to go with her, which surprised Jessie a little. Delilah was usually big on the girl stuff. But if she didn't want to come along, that would make things simpler.

Teddy nodded, only half hearing. Jessie made her way toward the rest rooms. Coming into Lori's earlier, she had suppressed her disgust as her flip flops stuck and pulled loose from the floor with each step. Now she barely noticed.

Inside the women's room she glanced around. Just to make sure, she stooped and checked under the door of each stall. Unless someone was standing on a toilet, she had the place to herself.

She needed to make this fast. Delilah could change her mind, and Teddy was capable of the odd attack of paranoia. He might bull his way right in here. She speed-dialed a phone number filed under "Janice" in her contacts.

"Hey, Jess," said a woman's voice. It was always a woman. Teddy might be listening, and she couldn't have a man answering her friend Janice's number.

"Green," said Jessie.

It was the color of the day. If she didn't work it into whatever she said, they would come running to get her out of trouble.

"What's up?" said Detective Ronald Tedeschi.

"Teddy's going to Mexico. I can go if you want me to."

"Damn, that's huge."

She could almost hear him thinking over the airwaves.

"I told you something like this could happen, but I didn't really think it would. This is going to go interagency."

Which meant more opportunities for bureaucratic fuckups.

"When?"

"Soon." She said." Any day."

"I'll set something up. Can you get away?"

"I can always go shopping."

"Damn," said Tedeschi again. "This is where we find out what you're made of. You'll be pretty much on your own."

I'm counting on it, Jessie thought.

That was the one thing she couldn't tell anyone.

3

CURLED UP ON HIS LEFT SIDE, Teddy snored. He had dropped the tough-guy front he showed the world, and she saw the little boy he had once been. That wasn't something she could afford to consider, not if she wanted to keep her focus on putting him in prison.

But sometimes she couldn't avoid thinking about it. Everyone she met in this new life, every dealer, user, enforcer, or hooker, had been a child. The difference was, she never saw them sleeping.

She slid out of bed and stood naked on the small patch of floor. She usually slept naked anyway, and Teddy wouldn't have had it any other way last night.

Outside was still darkness, but the usual rapid island transition to daylight would come any minute. Jessie picked Teddy's T-shirt up from the floor and pulled it over her head. She stooped again and found her cell phone in the tangle of her clothes. She headed down the narrow hallway to the door of the trailer.

Jessie climbed down to the ground and took a seat in one of the plastic chairs under the awning that Teddy had attached to his trailer. She speed dialed another number from her contacts. Tedeschi had warned her about storing numbers from her real life, but she could trust her mother to give nothing away. Not that Mom was especially protective of her daughter. Mom never told anybody anything.

She would be up at this early hour. It came with owning a restaurant.

"Mom, it's Jessie."

Silence.

"Tell me about Mexico."

"Why?"

"Because I'm going."

"Why?"

"You know why."

"It's a big country."

"I have a name and a location. Nogales. That's the last information you have, right?"

"Twenty years ago."

"Well, somebody named Hosea is there, and he sounds right. I can't afford to miss the chance."

"Why do you care after all this time?"

"I never stopped caring. But like you said, Mexico is a big country. I couldn't search it all, but Nogales, maybe I can."

The daylight was complete. Soon Teddy would start rolling around in bed. He would lose the battle against the daylight, and he would want her there when he awoke.

"I'll tell you how it goes," said Jessie.

She ended the call, before her mother could ruin it with something along the lines of, "Whatever."

4

HIGH TEA at the Veranda.

Jessie had to give them credit for imagination. An upscale Waikiki hotel was the last place to worry about running into Teddy Dias or any of his crew. Although, if Teddy ever saw the young women servers in their prim-necked blouses, long skirts and white gloves, he would want to dress her in an outfit like that just to rip it off her again.

That might be fun.

"It's not ideal," said the man called Ovitz.

He meant the plan, not the setting. The shade of an enormous banyan tree kept the temperature perfect.

Was he the DEA guy? No, the other one, who looked like an aging surfer, was from the DEA. His name was Paulaner. Ovitz was FBI, and he wore one of the few business suits to be seen on the streets of Honolulu.

"Meaning," said Tedeschi, "you would prefer your own agent in this assignment. We get that."

His tone was complacent as he prepared to play his ace.

"But Officer Hokoana is the one who got next to Teddy Dias."

"Azucar is federal business."

"It's not like we were poaching. We didn't make this case about Azucar. Dias did."

"We have people who are trained for this," said Ovitz.

"Believe it or not," said Tedeschi, "Honolulu P.D, has been known to do some undercover work. When we're not hoisting mai tais on the beach."

Ovitz turned to Jessie. Until that moment she hadn't been sure that he knew she was there.

"No offense intended, but you're improvising. Indications are, you have the instincts. But this is a huge case, and you have, what, two years on the job?"

"It's not my first undercover assignment," she couldn't resist saying.

"Which brings us back where we started," said Tedeschi. "Jessie has the in. We can't just hand off to some guy in a hula skirt. Dias will probably notice."

"I would," said Paulaner with a smile that he meant to be charming. It was, to a point.

He turned serious.

"I'm concerned about Chuey Almodovar. What's your take? Was this really a chance meeting, or a set-up?"

Jessie didn't need to think about that one.

"It was real. Chuey's not smart enough to hang back and make somebody come to him. It was Teddy's idea all the way."

"Where did you meet him?"

He knew that, but he wanted to hear it again.

"On the whale-watching cruise."

"Doesn't sound like Dias's kind of thing."

"It wasn't. That's why I'm sure it was coincidence, meeting Chuey. I was doing my flighty female act. 'Oh, Teddy, I've never seen a whale. Be a big strong man and show me a whale.' He complained about behaving like a *malihini*, but he did it for me."

"Then what?"

"Teddy didn't care about whales. Chuey didn't either. I was making girl talk with Chuey's girlfriend and trying to listen in. I could tell exactly when Teddy realized that Chuey is Azucar's nephew. He practically came in his pants."

Jessie suppressed a smile when Ovitz gave her a look of prim disapproval.

"He knew about Azucar?" said Paulaner.

"Definitely It's a weird hero-worship kind of thing. Teddy wants to be Azucar. Or maybe his son or something."

"Back-up is going to have to be very loose," said Ovitz as if Jessie and the DEA man hadn't spoken. "You'll be pretty much out there alone."

"We've discussed that," said Tedeschi.

"We'll be clearing it with a few people on the Mexican side, but there aren't many of them we can trust with the information. And they have to watch their backs with their own people."

It struck Jessie that none of the men had commented on how she had gotten close to Teddy Dias. Was it gallantry, or did they want deniability? Or least plausible of all, did they believe that Teddy Dias kept her around just to be decorative?

She stifled an urge to say, "For the record, I'm fucking him. If that's a problem for the case, we should talk about it now."

That was for the brass to worry about. She had enough on her plate.

5

"U.S. CITIZENS?" said the border guard.

"Yes," said Teddy for both of them.

Jessie had expected more scrutiny, but then she remembered that the guard had seen people from Hawaii before. Las Vegas wasn't that far away

The guard handed their drivers' licenses back to Teddy. Teddy kept his and passed Jessie's to her. She glanced to make sure he hadn't mixed them up. She felt the usual split second of alarm at the unfamiliar surname under her photograph.

It was time to stop that. It was past time, but every day her mental exhaustion grew. Someday it might make her blurt something fatal.

Teddy drove a couple of hundred yards into the Mexican Nogales, but his speed kept dropping. Jessie could tell he was holding up traffic, and a moment later the horns started blaring. She glanced at his face and saw the tight mask that meant he was confused. He hated to show it.

It was his first time away from Hawaii. Hers too, but she would have to take command without letting him realize it.

That was her first task. The second would be to shake off her federal backup and still hook up with Chuey.

And all on unfamiliar territory.

Retail shops, most of them tiny, lined both sides of the street. A rung below them on the economic ladder were the vendors working from push carts. Lowest of the low were the hucksters who carried their wares on trays slung from their necks.

"Teddy, this is heaven," said Jessie. "This is the major leagues of shopping."

Teddy grunted. His eyes still roved, searching for something familiar. He didn't find it.

"All that stuff to buy is calling me," she said.

"We have to find Chuey. And Frank."

Teddy's bodyguard was somewhere behind them. Teddy had figured that a couple and a single man would look less conspicuous than a mismatched trio.

"Let Chuey wait. What else can he do? Frank too. Look, there's a parking place."

A twenty-year-old Taurus had just lurched out in front of them. Teddy was so desperate for a respite that he swerved into the space that the other car had vacated. Before he stopped, Jessie had her door open and was halfway out of the car. She turned back.

"Come on. My wallet is itching."

Teddy slid after her. If she had a plan, he would go along.

Jessie pulled him into the nearest storefront. There was no theme to the merchandise. It covered everything from toys to cosmetics to kitchen utensils. Jessie grabbed a few lipsticks at random and laid them down on the counter.

"How much?"

"Dollars?"

"Sure."

"Three."

Jessie already had her wallet in her hand. She thumbed three singles out and laid them next to the merchandise. The pockmarked middle-aged man looked disappointed with her for skipping the haggling, but he took the money.

"You have a back door?"

"Yes, but it's nasty out there."

"That's okay."

She grabbed Teddy again. As she towed him toward the rear, she realized that the entire transaction had taken place in English.

This wasn't Mexico or the U.S. It was the border.

The man was right. The alley reeked, and Jessie didn't want to look down at what her shoes were picking up.

"What about the car?" said Teddy.

"We don't need it. That's why we bought a junker, remember?"

"How do we find Chuey?"

Good question.

"I have a feeling people know him here. We'll ask."

6

JESSIE LED TEDDY down the alley until it ran into a side street. Rather than go back to the same main street where they had left the car, she turned left. Teddy followed. She had never seen him so docile.

It took no more than three minutes to reach another thoroughfare lined with businesses. To the right she saw a small plaza with a dry fountain that seemed to serve as a local meeting place. She caught herself giving her best flat-eyed glare to a half dozen young men who idled there. She made herself look away. Teddy didn't like it when she looked as if she could take care of herself.

It also wouldn't help to act like a cop.

She had a feeling that the young men would know Azucar and his nephew, but they might also play for a rival team. A legitimate businessman who just wanted to get along might be her best bet for information.

Make that a businesswoman. The nearest shop was a

florist, and the mostly European-looking fifty-something woman behind the counter gave them a welcoming smile that vanished at Jessie's first words. If the woman hadn't been taken by surprise, she would have pretended to speak only Spanish.

"We are supposed to meet Chuey Almodovar, but we have become separated. Where can we find him?"

The woman was unwilling to commit.

"Senor Azucar will be grateful, I'm sure. And I'm sure his gratitude is useful."

"A moment, please," said the woman.

She disappeared into the back. Jessie assumed she was calling the local fixer. Any neighborhood in a Mexican city would have one.

The woman returned.

"Please go to the plaza and wait."

She didn't need to add, "And never come here again." Her face said it all.

So Jessie and Teddy would have to pass the scrutiny of the young men anyway.

They left the florist's shop and crossed the street. They didn't hurry, but they still arrived at the plaza with plenty of time for picking a fight. This was Teddy's element, and Jessie nudged him.

"Don't start anything."

"I'm no idiot."

No, but too much down time could make him forget. He wasn't the only problem, either. Her federal minders were frantically criss-crossing the city looking for her. She felt bad about that, but they would be more likely to get her killed than to help her.

All of which left her feeling exposed. Jessie exhaled when a dusty late-model Mercedes rounded the corner and stopped. She hadn't realized that she was holding her breath. The young men saw the car, and the tension broke. Jessie bent over to look at the driver.

"Delilah," she said. "Howzit?"

"Welcome to Mexico," said Delilah.

She waved at the young men, who were too cool to wave back.

"Let's go."

"Sorry for the mix up," said Jessie a few minutes later.

She was in the front seat with Delilah. Teddy sat in back and ignored the scenery, as he tried to recoup his macho. It wouldn't take long.

"It happens," said Delilah. "The border can be tricky."

So could shaking Feds from multiple agencies, but Jessie didn't plan to mention that part.

"Anyway, you're here, which is good. We've been working hard to make this deal happen."

"We?" said Jessie.

"Chuey has," said Delilah.

She glanced at Jessie with a clear message. The drug business was the most testosterone-fueled industry in an already male-dominated culture. They both needed to keep their fingerprints off the deal, or it wouldn't happen.

"Where we going?" said Jessie. "To meet Senor Azucar?"

"Not yet. Right now you settle in, relax. He'll let us know."

2

NOGALES WASN'T WEARING WELL.

It was only three days since Jessie had arrived, but it felt like months. She didn't think she had never seen anything as desperate as the endless hovels in the hills outside the town. Hawaii had its squalor and sadness, but there the sun warmed and soothed. Here the harsh light leaned on the earth until it would have groaned, if only it had the strength.

The other Nogales, the one in Arizona, didn't help. It looked almost close enough to touch, like prosperous people in an apartment across a narrow street.

Teddy Dias reclined in an aging armchair and watched the smoke from yet another joint as it clung to the ceiling of the apartment. The foreign sights and sounds and smells that made Jessie want to sob and run for home didn't seem to affect Teddy at all.

Frank looked even less impressed with his surroundings, which impressed Jessie. She knew that Teddy's bodyguard had never left Hawaii before. This might even be his first time off Oahu.

Their hostess still hadn't said a word. It was obvious to Jessie that no one had given the tiny middle-aged Mexican woman a choice about opening her home to the three *norteamericanos*.

That was another thing. To Jessie, *norteamericano* sounded like *malihini*.

Mainlander. At best, the term meant a character flaw to be overlooked.

Three knocks sounded on the door to the hallway. Frank peeled himself off the wall and reached inside his jacket. The door opened, and Chuey entered. Frank relaxed a little. Teddy still hadn't moved.

"It's tonight," Chuey said.

He threw his arms wide in a gesture that Jessie had seen too often. Chuey congratulated himself extravagantly for every small thing he accomplished.

"Uncle Porfirio will see us tonight at the fights."

He turned to the woman and fired some orders in Spanish. She didn't look pleased, but she nodded.

"Fights?" said Jessie.

She knew her tone lacked enthusiasm, but she didn't care. She had a good idea what kind of fights Chuey was talking about. Many people in Mexico made a living by supplying things that were harder to find north of the border.

Teddy let his head roll toward her on the armchair.

"We're guests here," he said. "If Mr. Azucar wants to watch the fights, we'll watch the fights."

At dusk the tiny woman fed them a spicy beef stew. Jessie already understood how things worked here. It was early for *comido*, the evening meal, but Mexicans knew that *norteamericanos* didn't do these things the civilized way. But the stew was tangy and satisfying, and Jessie wished she had the words to say she enjoyed it.

"*Mole de ollo,*" said the woman with a faint smile.

Jessie smiled back. She should have realized that this woman was someone's mother, and a mother knew when her efforts pleased.

Hawaiians are daylight people. Jessie was thinking longingly of a bed, any bed, when a vehicle horn sounded briefly outside.

"That's for us," said Chuey.

Frank checked the hallway and then started down the stairs. A moment later he whistled all clear. Chuey's impatience threatened to set his clothes on fire.

"Teddy, your homey don't have to check everything. If I say it's okay, it's okay."

"I know, Chuey. Humor him, okay? He takes my money. He wants to earn it."

That was Teddy, Jessie had learned. When he felt like it, he could charm.

Chuey led Teddy and Jessie downstairs, where a Jeep Cherokee waited. The driver said nothing as they climbed in. He looked as if he spent a lot of time saying nothing. In his world it was a survival skill.

"Delilah's not coming?" said Jessie.

Chuey hesitated.

"She don't like the fights."

Jessie said nothing, but the news puzzled her. This was Delilah's deal as much as Chuey's. Jessie wouldn't have trusted Chuey to get it right, and she was surprised that Delilah did.

The silent man drove further into the hills, away from the center of Nogales. After a while the terrain smoothed, and the darkness became total. The universe could have disappeared except for the strip of two-lane highway pinned in their headlights.

Jessie would have felt relieved when a pool of light appeared on their left, but she knew that it meant the next step in her ordeal. The driver turned left abruptly and left the road. Jessie hadn't seen any kind of landmark. Maybe it didn't matter where they turned. At some point the land had turned as flat as a dinner plate.

As they approached, the lighted area grew and became a cluster of ranch buildings. The most conspicuous was a huge barn-like structure. The driver headed straight for the building. He flashed his high beams four times, three short and one long. As he maintained his steady fifteen miles per hour, a gap appeared in the side of the barn. The sliding door continued to open as the Jeep rolled inside and stopped.

"*Senor* Azucar is here?" she said. "It looks pretty conspicuous."

That could be a problem. Her Feds might be here, hoping to pick up her trail again.

Chuey gave her a superior chuckle.

"Right about now the Army is getting reports about him being someplace else completely. Only the CI they think is theirs is really working for us, see?"

"I get it."

The driver stayed behind the wheel. Chuey climbed out of the front passenger seat and opened the right rear door. Frank got out first and turned to help Jessie. Teddy followed. Jessie stood, disoriented. Harsh shouts bounced around the steel innards of the building and assaulted her ears. Pungent male smells crowded in on her. Rows of lights powerful enough for an airport runway blinded her for a moment.

She looked away. When her eyes recovered, the first thing that drew them was a structure within the structure. It looked like a cage, and she realized it was exactly that. And she knew what kind of fights she had come to see. The stew in her stomach gurgled and lurched. She kept it down, but the spices she had enjoyed earlier punished her now.

You are a police officer, she told herself. You can do what you have to do.

Chuey pointed into the steel bleachers surrounding all four sides of the cage. He started climbing and seemed to assume that Jessie and Teddy would follow. There wasn't much choice.

Men leered at Jessie as she climbed over them or brushed past, making futile attempts to avoid touching them. Teddy was usually tiresome about men who paid her this kind of attention, but he knew this wasn't his territory. He couldn't afford to make enemies.

That was why he put a restraining hand on Frank's shoulder three times before they reached their seats.

Every step that Jessie climbed increased her dread. Chuey had told them they would be honored guests. It was a bad sign that they were bleacher trash, and worse that Chuey had everything so wrong.

She heard hoarse hectoring from the cage behind her, and by the time she had turned back toward the announcer's voice and taken her seat, the first fight had started between two small, wiry men of mostly Indian ancestry.

She pretended to watch while paying as little attention as she could. So many parts of the human body were good for nothing but bleeding.

"Tomato cans," said Teddy with disgust in his tone.

He always enjoyed explaining things to her, and she usually played to his ego. This time she couldn't force herself to fake it. He went on anyway.

"Guys who get paid to bleed. They spring a leak like a

tomato can and in a couple of days they're as good as new. We can see this anyplace."

"If we really want to."

Teddy scowled, and Jessie told herself to be careful. This wasn't the place to show him a new side of herself.

The fighters got bigger each bout. Some of them were more skilled with their fists and feet and elbows, and more adept with a thumb to the eye. Others were just bigger tomato cans.

The announcer entered the cage again. Instead of launching right into his spiel, he paused for drama. Chuey leaned across Teddy and spoke to Jessie.

"This is the big one. The main event. Just wait."

The announcer started shouting in Spanish. He had shredded his voice by now, but he pushed it even harder. Jessie winced, as he own throat ached in sympathy.

A fighter approached the cage through the gap between two bleachers across from Jessie. He looked like slabs of muscle barely contained by his skin.

"Give it up for Sergei the Assassin!"

The crowd cheered and yelled, but the fighter didn't acknowledge the commotion.

Chuey leaned toward Teddy and Jessie.

"He's Russian. For real. That's not just a stage name. They have to go all over the world for fighters to go up against Hosea."

Hosea?

Jessie almost blurted the name back at Chuey.

Another man appeared, much like the first except for even more scar tissue that turned his face into a mask.

"And welcome Bonecrusher Barak, the Siberian tiger!"

Instead of facing each other, the two men crossed the cage floor and stopped side by side, facing the entrance to the cage.

A full minute passed. In the crowd someone started stomping on the metal bleachers. Other spectators took up the rhythm. The sound of stressed metal spread around the huge space. Jessie began to bounce on her bench, and she started to imagine the bleacher collapsing. She grabbed for Teddy in a near panic.

But then the reckless stomping tapered off and turned to shouting and hand clapping. Jessie looked. A man approached the cage. Jessie knew she was gaping, but she couldn't help it. This was what she had come for. Her under-cover assignment was the pretext. This was the real thing. Why was she so astonished?

The man was huge, even bigger than the first two. And he was Hawaiian, more Hawaiian than she was.

The shouting of the crowd reached its maximum. No one heard Jessie's single word.

"Daddy."

She knew him. She hadn't seen him for twenty years, but she knew her own father, didn't she? Not even Teddy heard her. At this point he wouldn't have cared.

8

THE ANNOUNCER SCREAMED some more into the microphone. Jessie heard none of it. She stared at the scar on her father's left side. That was something she didn't remember at all.

Her own torso wouldn't have had room for the intricate pattern of old pain, but on him it looked like a shaving cut.

The announcer finished screaming and backed out of the cage. The first two men split up. One moved around Hosea's right flank, while the other went to his left. Hosea didn't react, except to let a smile appear in his face. His two opponents obviously planned to circle him and take turns attacking him from behind, as he tried to deal with one or the other.

The cop in Jessie recognized the danger. She wanted to scream at him to watch his back. Never let anyone slip behind you, not even someone who seems to pose no threat.

And these two men defined the word threat.

The two opponents began to circle Hosea. He moved to the center of the ring and considerately gave them room to maneuver. He started to rotate in the opposite direction. Jessie saw his strategy. Either was welcome to attack him from behind, but the other would be the first to pay the price. They had to decide between them.

The crowd had fallen silent, but now protests began to come from the bleachers.

Sergei launched himself at Hosea's back. He landed one, two, three kidney punches, as Barak attacked from the front. Hosea stood him up straight with a right fist to the jaw. The punch was almost too fast to see, as was his right elbow as he threw it into reverse and hammered Sergei's temple.

Both men staggered under the one-two, but they refused to fall. Hosea showed Barak his back as he threw a left into Sergei's midsection. Sergei fell and rolled away in desperation.

Hosea whirled again and jabbed with his left, but Barak reversed out of range. He stopped and approached Hosea at an angle. Jessie saw his strategy. He meant to maneuver Hosea toward Sergei on the floor, who could then attack from below.

Again Hosea seemed to cooperate. He backed away from Barak, but just as he was about to stray too close to the opponent on the floor, Hosea darted forward and grabbed Barak by the shoulder and the waistband of his shorts. He heaved the man off the floor and over his head. Hosea spun and brought the man down hard on top of his partner. Both Russians appeared done for the night, but Hosea stood over them for a moment to make sure.

Jessie missed it, along with everyone else in the arena. The first thing she saw was the cage door flapping. She hadn't seen it open. A third man had come from nowhere to loom behind her father.

"Daddy," she screamed, but everyone else was screaming as well. Not even Teddy heard her.

The third man braced his right fist against his left palm and drove his right elbow into the bone behind Hosea's ear. The new opponent was big enough to reach his target, and to make the blow count. Hosea dropped and landed face down between the other two men. The new man followed, landing with both knees on Hosea's back.

The third man circled his arm around Hosea's throat in a choke hold. The two Russians roused themselves enough to punch Hosea from both sides.

Ground and pound. Jessie had heard the term from fans of extreme fighting. The brutality in the term became clear to her now.

Hosea ignored the fists that kept landing from both sides. He drew one of his knees up under his chest, and then the other. His face showed that the choke hold was taking effect, and he didn't have much time before the lights went out.

With an extra three hundred pounds on his back, Hosea levered himself to his feet. He reached up over his head. His hands easily circled the third man's twenty-inch neck. Hosea yanked on the man and ducked hard. The man flew off Hosea's back and landed hard on his own. Hosea kicked the man in the jaw, and it was over.

Hosea stood alone in the carnage, and the noise that made Jessie wonder whether she would ever hear normally again. The announcer ventured back into the cage with the microphone and held up his hand. He waited for several minutes, but realized that yelling would be wasted effort. He raised Hosea's hand to signal victory.

Jessie felt tears come to her eyes. The announcer was holding onto one of Hosea's fingers instead of his wrist, which was too big to grip. Twenty years fell away, and Jessie reached straight up as if to take her father's little finger. She lowered her arm and looked around, but no one in the bleachers had noticed her gesture.

Hosea raised his other arm over his head and made a slow turn to salute the entire arena. He left the cage, as his three opponents began to stir on the floor. No one seemed concerned about them. The noise of the crowd dwindled and disappeared. Only a hollow numbness in Jessie's ears remained.

"That's the whole card," Chuey said.

His voice seemed to come from a distance.

Chuey got up from his seat, along with most of the spectators. The crowd began to break up and move down the bleachers like chunks of brand new rock falling from a lava flow as it ran out of heat and momentum.

Jessie approved of the metaphor in more ways than one. The temperature of the huge space seemed to come from the earth's core.

Some of the men and even more of the women looked riled up and ready for more blood and pain. There might be impromptu match-ups outside, with the women inciting their men or even getting into it themselves.

Others turned listless and exhausted. Jessie sympathized, and she wished she could just go home, as they planned to do.

Chuey looked more excited now than he had during the fights.

"Now we find my uncle."

He led the way against the flow of the crowd to the corridor that the fighters had used to reach the cage.

Jessie realized that they were heading for a locker room. She had more than enough experience with locker rooms.

They encouraged the male of the species at his worst. That went for her colleagues in the police, too.

The four of them made slow progress, but finally they reached end of the corridor. Jessie saw that "locker room" overstated the case. She found herself in a room with a packed dirt floor and little else but a few grimy plastic chairs and a wooden table in the far corner. Next to the table a middle-aged man sat on a steel folding chair that his subordinates probably carried wherever they went. The man wore a gray tropical gray suit that Jessie estimated as a trim 38 regular. The temperature was only slightly lower in this room, but the man seemed comfortable. He glanced from his nephew to Teddy to Jessie. He ignored Frank, as if he recognized and dismissed hired muscle in the same moment. He kept his eyes on Jessie, as he spoke in Spanish into a cell phone. The man kept talking, and Jessie knew he was making a point of his rudeness.

Finally he ended the call.

"Uncle Porfirio," Chuey said. He started forward with his arms outstretched for a traditional embrace, but his uncle's demeanor made his stop uncertainly.

"Nephew," said the man in American-accented English.

He must be another product of the border region.

An awkward silence followed. Four of Porfirio Azucar's underlings stood along the wall behind him. None of them spoke or moved.

"Uncle, these are my friends from Hawaii. I told you about them."

Another pause.

"Refresh my memory," said Azucar.

This was not going well.

"My vacation. I told you, we met them. Me and Delilah. They have great product in Hawaii, especially on the Big

Island. They call it *pakalolo*. Kona Gold, Puna Butter. They're legendary."

He waited for encouragement, but none came.

"My idea is, we can add a new line to our business. Top of the line product at top prices. Teddy can fix us up."

"Do we need help in our own business?"

"No, Uncle, we don't need help. But we don't mind making money, do we?"

Chuey tried a smile, which his uncle didn't return.

"We also care about security," said Azucar. "Which to my mind means keeping things in the family. I recall telling you this."

Azucar spoke a few words in Spanish over his right shoulder. The man on the far right reached inside his windbreaker.

Frank knew what the movement meant. He went for his gun, but he was one man against too many, and their teamwork was too smooth. While Frank tried to deal with the wrong threat, the man on the far left shot him.

"We're guests," Jessie recalled Teddy saying. "Guests don't bring a whole team of bodyguards. Shows lack of trust."

A little lest trust might have helped. It might have kept them from coming here in the first place.

She had no right to blame Teddy, though. It should have sent her running for the border when Delilah didn't join the party. Azucar had allowed Jessie into his all-male party only because he planned to kill her.

She vomited the reeking remains of her dinner. If she lived, she would never eat anything but the blandest food she could find.

That was a big if.

No one reacted, not Azucar, not his men, and not Teddy. The others didn't care. Teddy couldn't afford the distraction. Jessie saw his gun hand flex and start toward the weapon that he had left behind. He remembered, and his hand dropped to his side.

At that moment the door to the small room opened, and the winner of the last fight came in. The huge man looked around the room. His eyes rested on Jessie for just a moment, but she knew he had taken in everything about her.

That meant he had recognized the Hawaiian in her, as she had seen it in him. But what else did he see? He was the man she remembered, but she was no longer a little girl.

"Wait outside, please, Hosea," said Azucar. "Excellent fight tonight."

"Thanks," said Hokoana. "Oh, and thanks for the little surprise."

Azucar's smile held no hint of apology.

"Things were getting a little routine, don't you think, Hosea? The fans need a little novelty now and then."

"If you mean you wanted me to lose, they didn't get it."

"True."

Hosea folded his arms and stayed where he was. He glanced at Frank's body on the floor, but he had seen such things before.

Azucar gave him a warning look, but Hosea had a way of shrugging without moving. Azucar spoke more Spanish to his man.

"Now, Hosea," said Azucar.

"Okay," said Hokoana after a provocative pause.

He took his eyes from Jessie and turned to go. Jessie wondered why she couldn't move or speak. She realized that she didn't want to get her father killed. He wasn't bulletproof.

Then it was too late. Hosea disappeared.

The first underling to Azucar's right reached behind his back. His hand came back into view holding a Glock pistol, which he handed to his boss. Jessie's bad feeling got worse.

Azucar hefted the gun in his right hand and nodded.

"You are an idiot," he told Chuey. "But you are also my sister's son. I can do nothing about you except teach you a lesson."

He held the gun out toward Chuey.

"Take this. Take your friends outside and kill them. Paco and Esteban will go with you to make sure you have no more brilliant ideas."

9

THIS IS HOW IT ENDS, Jessie thought.

Her brilliant police career and her life were history. No one at home would know what had happened or where to find her body. She would never rest at home.

Regret instead of terror. Was it a better way to die?

She glanced at Teddy and a thrill of admiration cut through her. He met Azucar's eyes with his own. Jessie knew he wouldn't beg or blame Chuey.

In that moment she loved Teddy Dias, and the drug dealing and pimping that came with the package. And if she didn't survive to carry out her assignment and betray him, maybe that wasn't such a bad thing.

"Go," Azucar said.

He added a flip of his hand, and the contempt in the gesture shocked Jessie out of her lethargy. The two underlings pushed themselves away from the wall and started toward her and Teddy. As Jessie turned to go, her eyes flicked across

Teddy's. His hand brushed hers and passed her a message.

Follow my lead. Do what I do.

She didn't need words to understand. That was what love did.

But there was still the question of what they could do against armed men. Jessie hoped there might still be spectators milling outside and arguing over what they had seen, but Azucar's security team ran a tight operation. They had chased everyone away, and only hard dirt remained where hundreds of vehicles had parked.

There was no one to witness, but Azucar's men seemed to feel that murder and darkness went together. One of them pointed to the right. Again Chuey led the way around the side of the building.

A little light bled around the corner from the front of the building. The man called Paco stopped right on the edge of the shadow. He pointed at the corrugated metal wall.

"Go over there," he said. "We'll make it quick."

Instead of cooperating, Teddy charged. He moved fast, but not fast enough. Paco hammered him with his heavy steel flashlight. Teddy fell to his hands and knees and tried to shake the grogginess off. Jessie knew she had let Teddy down. She hadn't even twitched.

"Let's try that again," said Paco.

Jessie crouched next to Teddy and massaged his shoulders. Shame at her pathetic ministrations turned her throat dry.

"Up," said Paco.

"Fuck you," said Jessie. "If you're going to shoot, shoot. Don't expect us to help."

"Whatever you say. Chuey?"

Chuey had been standing by, dreading his part in the scenario.

"Move, Chuey, or you can join them."

Azucar had said he couldn't kill his sister's son, but Chuey wasn't thinking clearly enough to remember. He stepped closer to Jessie and Teddy, but his gun hand still hung next to his thigh.

"Last chance, Chuey."

Chuey raised the gun. Jessie couldn't be sure in the near darkness, but she thought she saw his eyes close. This could get messy, but Paco and Esteban were on hand to clean it up.

Jessie watched Chuey's hand. Fascination chased terror from her mind.

A mobile mountain appeared behind Chuey. Hosea Hokoana lifted Chuey off his feet and threw him to the side. The young man fell heavily on his back, and Jessie heard his breath leave him. Whatever happened next, Chuey was out of it.

Hosea turned just as Paco chopped at his wrist with the flashlight. Jessie heard metal thump on meat, but Hosea ignored the impact. He knocked the flashlight aside and hammered Paco's jaw with his other fist. Paco did a flawless back dive, but he made a thud instead of a splash.

That left Esteban, but he weighed his chances and turned to run deeper into the darkness. Hosea stooped and picked up Paco's flashlight. He threw it after Esteban. The heavy cylinder turned end over end as it faded from sight. Jessie heard another solid impact, a grunt, and a falling body.

Hosea looked around for something else to entertain him. When he saw nothing, he stood as if he wouldn't need to move again in this life.

Jessie realized that she was still holding Teddy's shoulders. She helped him to his feet. He made it, but he leaned against her.

Hosea nodded at Jessie.

"Where you from?"

"Molokai," Jessie said before she could think about it.

That was cover story her police handlers had given her. What was she? Daughter? Lover? Cop? All-around liar?

"Why did you help us?"

Hosea shrugged.

"Not sure. Homesick, maybe."

"But you knew what they were going to do."

"I heard them talking. I don't speak Spanish with them, and they think I can't. Makes them careless."

"I guess you don't want to work for Azucar anymore."

"I never liked him. We need to get going."

Hosea walked over to Chuey and nudged him with his foot. Chuey looked able to stand but unwilling to get back in the game.

"You with us?"

"I better stick around," said Chuey.

The clueless optimism had left his tone, leaving nothing but self-contempt. Jessie almost felt sorry for him.

"You need to make some time for us to get started," said Hosea. "Understand? You owe us that much."

"Yeah. You want my Jeep?"

"Appreciate the offer," said Hosea, "but then they'll know what to look for."

He took out a cell phone and checked it. "What do you know? A signal out here."

Hosea speed dialed and said in English, "I need a vehicle. Big enough for me. With the usual equipment. You know where to meet me."

He ended the call. "Come on. We can use my car for a little while. Long enough."

Hosea pointed at a large SUV, almost invisible in the darkness just fifty feet away. He started toward it without checking whether anyone was following. Jessie helped Teddy along, but his strength was returning.

"I guess we go with him," said Teddy. "Not much choice. Hold on a second."

He stopped leaning on her shoulder and detoured over the Chuey. Before Jessie realized what Teddy intended, he kicked Chuey in the ribs. Chuey absorbed the punishment in silence, as if he deserved it.

"You didn't need to do that," said Jessie.

"Yeah, I did. It's a matter of principle."

Bickering was part of love, wasn't it? She didn't have much practice.

Hosea was behind the wheel, waiting. Jessie watched Teddy climb into the back seat and then got in next to her father.

Her father. Was she going to say anything about that, or just act her cover story? At some point she would have to find out.

It felt strange being a spectator in her own life.

Hosea put the vehicle in gear and drove off into darkness. When the illumination from the fight arena had dwindled and disappeared, he turned his headlights on. They didn't reveal much more than featureless desert, but he seemed to know where he was.

The desert looked flatter than it was. The vehicle bounced mercilessly, and Jessie feared that if she tried to speak, her teeth would sever her tongue.

That was as good an excuse as any for saying nothing.

She still hadn't seen any kind of landmark, but the headlights picked up another SUV, this one a Toyota Sequoia. She hoped it differed enough from the Excursion to fool their pursuers for a while. Hosea needed large vehicles, and Azucar knew that.

Hosea didn't give the Excursion a farewell look as he went to the Sequoia. Again Jessie and Teddy followed. Again they drove west over desert terrain, until daylight appeared behind them and overtook them. Hosea was watching for something. He grunted with satisfaction. At first Jessie couldn't imagine what there was to please him, but then she saw it—a long strip of ground scraped even flatter by a bulldozer's blade.

"They fly in here once a day," he said. "Shouldn't be long."

"Who's 'they?' And who are these people helping us?"

"Different people I worked with now and then. They owe me favors."

Jessie's answer fled her mind, as she noticed a mini-parade of three Escalades materializing out of the heat shimmer that was already settling on the desert. At the same time she heard a snarling engine overhead. A two-engine prop plane executed a half-circle to align itself with the airstrip. But instead of landing, the pilot pulled into another tight circle. He must have noticed the Escalades.

Hosea did too.

"I guess they're going to be a pain in the ass."

Men had already emerged from the Escalades. They held assault rifles, which they started firing before they had steadied themselves enough to be effective. Jessie recognized the rifles even at a distance. The AK-47 was a capable weapon, but at sniper range it wasn't much good.

She realized how much Azucar's men feared Hosea. They didn't want to get close to him.

Hosea climbed out of the driver's seat, and walked around the vehicle to the tailgate, which he lowered. He might have been unpacking for a pre-game barbecue, for all the concern he showed. He took something from the cargo space that proved to be a rifle of a different sort.

He lined up a shot, and Jessie saw one of Azucar's men flop backward and lie still. The other men scattered for cover. There wasn't much.

"You go with this plane," said Hosea.

"Me?"

"You and Teddy."

Hosea turned back and fired another shot. A man in a prone firing position let his rifle fall. Maybe he was dead, or maybe he was faking it, but the result was the same.

"If you're smart," said Hosea, "you'll split off from him. Meet up later if you have to."

That was more tactful than, "Dump him," but Jessie got the idea. She didn't give Hosea her opinion. She owed him.

But there was one question she couldn't let go.

"Why?"

"What what?"

"Why are you doing this for us?"

"I've been here too long. It's time for me to go back where I belong."

"You don't even know us."

"I don't have to. I know who you are."

"Really? Is that what you think?"

Jessie wasn't sure she had a right to this anger, after she had let so much time with him get away.

She started marching toward the airplane. Teddy fell into step beside her. The propeller noise grew rapidly as she approached. When she came close enough to see the pilot, she recognized him as a Fed—not one of her Feds, but by now she knew the species. It was another thing to make her wonder what her father had done for twenty years.

She turned, unsure whether Hosea Hokoana would even hear her.

"My name is Jessie," she yelled.

Hosea stood, as still and impassive as a mountain. Jessie turned and climbed into the plane.

"I'll see you back there," he said.

10

"IT'S IMPORTANT, JESSIE."

Detective Ronald Tedeschi looked at her over his coffee cup.

"This is a serious fuckup. You made the Feds look bad for losing you, and you didn't get results."

She didn't bother to answer.

"I need to know what happened, minute by minute. Teddy's lawyer will try to get her fingernails under something, and believe me, she's good. If there's something there, she'll find it."

"You knew I was going to be deep. They knew it too."

"We did, but I also thought you'd have something to show for it."

She and Tedeschi shared a table in Lappert's. He had bought small dishes of vanilla ice cream to pay the rent on their table, but both sat untouched. Outside, visitors and locals waged the usual parking wars in downtown Lahaina.

Tedeschi had insisted on meeting on Maui, which was awkward. Teddy wanted her with him, and he didn't understand why she had to get back on a plane already, just minutes after they had met up in Honolulu.

"*Ohana*," she had told him. "Haven't seen my mother in a while. She'll get worried and start poking into things."

Teddy gave her a strange look.

"You're from Molokai."

That's what undercover burnout and a near death experience did. She started making obvious mistakes.

"Why's your mother on Maui?"

"Shopping. It's genetic."

Maui was the big city to residents of Molokai. It had led to a time-consuming detour, to make sure Teddy bought the story. She still wasn't sure it had worked.

"I met Azucar," she told Tedeschi, "He did us the courtesy because of his nephew, but he blew us off in five minutes. He left."

"So Chuey couldn't deliver. What about the girlfriend? You sure that's all she is?"

"As opposed to what?"

"As opposed to in on the deal."

"I hardly saw her."

Tedeschi frowned and thought for several minutes.

"I'll have to bring this back to the brass and the prosecutor's office. But I have a feeling we're going to roll Teddy up. What we have is all we're going to get. That means we have to pull you out."

He went on, but Jessie couldn't make herself concentrate. "Pull you out" sounded too offhand for what it meant to her. It meant taking her away from Teddy, while they tried to send him to prison.

Tedeschi said something that seemed to require an

answer. All she could do was nod. He got up from the table and left. Jessie sat and toyed with her spoon. What time was her flight to Honolulu? She should have written it down.

Na, she should never write anything down. What was she thinking? This life was going to kill her. At the very least, it would destroy her career. If Tedeschi suspected that she had lied to him, he could verify it in minutes.

A huge form loomed over her. It seemed to have come from nowhere.

"You're too easy to find," said her father.

Jessie found that she couldn't look up, or speak.

"Do you really eat that stuff?" he said.

She looked at her soupy chocolate ice cream.

"Comfort food," she said. "I grew up on Spam and KFC."

"I know."

She didn't remember getting up, but now she was standing toe to toe with him. The fact that her nose pointed at his abdomen didn't intimidate her.

"No, you don't know. You weren't there."

"You're right," he said. "I'm sorry about that."

She stepped back enough to get a look at his face.

"You know who I am?" she said.

"You told me, remember?"

"But you knew before."

"I did. The minute I saw you."

"Why didn't you say anything?"

"I wasn't sure you knew. And I wasn't sure you would want to have anything to do with me."

Jessie looked around. They were starting to attract looks, and she had enough undercover instinct left to prevent that. She slipped back into her seat and looked at him expectantly. He followed and took a seat opposite her, although he barely fit between the bench and the table. He must have been uncomfortable, but Jessie already knew that her father never gave anything away.

"But then," Hosea said, "I realized. You must have come looking for me. Too much coincidence any other way."

That sentence told her something. She had a unique hold on him. Hosea Hokoana normally needed no help in drawing conclusions or deciding what to do.

"So," said her father, "what about Teddy Dias?"

"What about him? He's my boyfriend."

"He's also your objective."

She started. How could he know that?

"That man you just met with," said Hosea as if she had asked aloud. "I know a cop when I see one. You're either a confidential informant or a cop. I vote for cop. Even though nobody knows anything about you."

"You could get me killed."

"Relax. I know how to ask. And who."

"Teddy's still my boyfriend."

"Then you have a dilemma."

He paused and looked at her steadily, until she had an idea what was coming.

"If I was any kind of father, I would solve that problem for you. Make him go away."

She was already shaking her head.

"Way too late for that. If you want to be a father, you'll let me solve my own problems."

He nodded and got up without breaking the table. "Let's walk."

And just like that, she obeyed. They stepped out of the air conditioning into the mid-afternoon sun. There was a reason why every business on Front Street had an awning to crank down after lunch.

"Were you going to ask me about my mother?"

"Not right away. I was going to test the waters a little first. Okay, how is she?"

"I don't see her that much. I guess her life works for her. We had a lot of short-term stepfathers. Me and Abie."

"Abie?"

"My half-brother. I don't see much of him these days either."

"Your mother's entitled to a life. I didn't give her much of one."

"She's entitled to think of us a little now and then."

"What's Abie like?"

"He's a moke."

A tough guy with an attitude.

"So was I. Still am, I guess."

"That's what Mom said."

Without discussing it or even thinking about it, they crossed the street and found shade under the venerable banyan that covered a city block. Some of the regulars in the park were predators when the opportunity presented itself, but with her father it wouldn't.

"What did she tell you about why I left?" he said.

"She didn't tell me anything until years later. She might have thought I didn't remember you."

"But you did."

"But I did."

They walked.

"I got into a situation," he said. "Not a one on one kind of situation, or a three on one. I can handle that. But these guys, they didn't do fair fights."

"Is that where the scar comes from?"

"You could say that."

That was a strange way to put it, but he didn't look at things the way most people did.

"I didn't have a choice about leaving. But maybe I could have come back sooner."

She didn't know what it was in his tone, but she knew he was asking her for judgment. He would accept her verdict, no matter what it was.

They walked without speaking.

"How does it feel to be back?"

She couldn't quite make herself say, "Welcome home," but he accepted her words.

"Not sure yet. I'm easing my way back to Kauai. Then Ni'ihau, maybe. That would be the real test."

"I'm not Hawaiian enough to live on Ni'ihau."

"Then I won't either."

This time their silence lasted, and Jessie got a feeling, that he was about to invite her to do something that she might not want to do. The feeling reminded her of nothing so much as the apprehension she got when a young man girded himself to ask her on a date, and she wasn't sure she liked him "that way."

Talk about weird.

"I need to get right with the religion. I've been away from that, too. Got for make *ho'oponopono*."

"You can still speak pidgin."

"Like putting my own clothes back on. Feels good."

"Maybe that's my problem," she said. "Not sure which clothes are mine anymore."

"The religion is a good place to start. And things are happening on the Big Island," he said. "There's going to be a ritual at the volcano. You could come, if you want. Might make your situation clearer for you."

"Okay," she heard herself say.

"It could still be a few months. I'll let you know."

She could count on it. That much she knew.

OCTOBER

11

"THAT'S SOME CLOSE SURVEILLANCE you're doing there," Coutinho said.

"The safety of the undercover officer is of paramount concern," said Kim. "The manual says so."

"And we always go by the book."

"Plus, she's hot."

Coutinho peered over his partner's shoulder at Officer Hokoana's image on the laptop screen. The video feed from the front room showed her sitting on a cot and looking bored. She stretched her feet out in front of her in their open-toed sandals and examined her painted toenails. Her legs were excellent, strong but well-shaped. Her short shorts showed them clear to her hips, and her halter top didn't conceal much, either. Coutinho admired her strong breasts, but he also appreciated athletic shoulders like hers.

"She looks *hapa*," said Kim.

"She is. Hawaiian and Irish, according to her."

"Who's the *haole*?"

"Her mother," said Coutinho. "Her father was so Hawaiian, he was from Ni'ihau."

He meant the private island southwest of Kauai, where the owners allowed only native Hawaiians to live. The residents still went about their daily business in the Hawaiian language.

"That's pretty Hawaiian," Kim said.

"Her father had to leave Ni'ihau to marry her mother."

"How come you got to pick her up at the airport?"

"Rank hath its privileges. Plus, Tanaka trusted me to watch the bad guys instead of her tits."

"I'm a leg man."

"Whatever."

"Look alive," said a voice in Coutinho's earpiece.

He had been reminding himself to expect it, but he still jumped a little.

Lieutenant Tanaka was speaking from his observation post across the street. That was one thing about the recession. When the cops needed a location for a stakeout, they had their choice of vacant commercial properties in downtown Hilo.

"She has a john," Coutinho told Kim.

"Got him. The door's just opening."

The banter stopped, because the boredom that provoked it had vanished. This was the real thing. The man entering the front room might be a hapless tourist picking the wrong moment to get horny, or he could be the one who was stabbing and slashing his way through the prostitutes of Hilo. One woman was dead and another not far from it. The third had been lucky, and if she ever forgot, a glance at her scar would remind her.

"Two hundred dollars means it's just a john," said Kim.

"I remember."

"If she says three hundred, that means he's this entrepreneur we're looking for."

Coutinho didn't resent hearing it again. Minds could go blank under stress.

They could also wander. His was wondering where this moke had been. Nine months after hacking up Gladys Robles, the prostitute killer was back.

Later, Coutinho told himself.

Hokoana stood to greet the man who came into the picture.

"Know him?" said Kim in a low voice.

"No."

"Me neither."

That was a surprise. The man was an island mix of Portuguese and Filipino or Japanese. He was also a moke. Coutinho should have known him or at least recognized him, which suggested that he came from another island

If the average moke had two hundred dollars on him, there wouldn't be a W-2 form involved.

The man said something, quietly enough that the microphones between Hokoana's breasts transmitted only a murmur. Coutinho hoped the undercover remembered to speak up.

"Two hundred or three," Kim said again.

Or a kick in the balls. Hokoana went with that option, which Coutinho hadn't foreseen. The man doubled over. Hokoana followed up by clapping his ears with her open hands and poking him in the eyes with both index fingers. He dropped to the floor, and something fell onto the floor. The screen of the elderly laptop didn't have the highest resolution. Coutinho bent forward for a closer look.

"Shit!" he yelled.

The object on the floor was a knife. Hokoana stepped out of her high heeled sandals and sprinted out of the monitor frame.

Coutinho yanked his earpiece out and started to run to the undercover officer's aid, but Kim made it through the door first. As Coutinho piled into the room, his partner was already cuffing the stranger's hands behind his back. The john, or whatever he was, probably offered no threat. All he wanted to do was hug himself after Hokoana's tender care, but Kim was right to immobilize him. Police work was about making sure. And if the handcuffs bit too hard, the moke shouldn't have tried to stab a cop.

Coutinho hustled through the front room to the store's street entrance. Outside, Hokoana had regained control of herself. She stood barefoot on the sidewalk and hugged herself as if against a chill.

His cell phone rang.

"Is she okay?" said Lieutenant Tanaka.

"Think so. The moke had a knife, but she handled him."

"I'll be right down."

Three minutes later Lieutenant Tanaka joined the cluster of cops. He was tall for his ancestry. Coutinho always felt a little disoriented at the sight of a Japanese face six feet above the ground. Tanaka pointed at Hokoana and then at the open door. The undercover officer didn't need it explained to her. She went back inside.

The lieutenant turned to Coutinho and Kim.

"What's up with the john?"

"I guess he's our man."

"We'll ask him, when he can talk."

A couple of uniforms emerged from the storefront. Between them the john was walking unaided, but he didn't look happy with the way life was treating him. He wouldn't for some time.

Tanaka went inside. Coutinho blinked in surprise when the lieutenant came right back out.

"Did we have somebody on the back entrance?"

"Yeah," said Coutinho. "Those two uniforms who just took the john away."

"Figures," said Tanaka. "The way things are going today, it just figures. They won't be able to tell us which way she went."

"Went?" said Coutinho and immediately felt stupid.

"As in, she was there, but she's not there now."

Tanaka blew air out.

"What else could go wrong?"

The lieutenant's cell phone rang. He lifted the tail of his aloha shirt and fished the phone out of his pocket.

"What?"

His face took on the immobility that Coutinho knew as the lieutenant's version of rage. Tanaka listened for a while and snapped the phone shut.

"Uniforms just made a traffic stop up around Laupahoehoe."

Coutinho listened. There had to be more.

"The moke was going to get a ticket for a busted headlight, until he volunteered that we're looking for him. Seems he cut up a few hookers and feels just a little bit bad about it."

Kim had joined them in time to hear the report. All three cops processed the information for a moment.

"Do we believe him?" Coutinho said.

False confessions were always a possibility.

"Hell, yes. Wasn't I just wondering what else could go wrong?"

"So what was all this about?"

"I was hoping Hokoana could illuminate us."

12

BEFORE COUTINHO COULD START processing the john, Tanaka called him into his office. Kim took over the booking chores. Tanaka kept Coutinho standing in front of his desk.

"Let's go through what you and the undercover talked about on the way from the airport."

"You going to call her boss?"

"Not yet. I would prefer to be able to explain what the fuck is going on."

"We can't sit on it for long," said Coutinho.

"As long as we can."

"I don't know much more than you. Honolulu P.D., two years on the job. She passed the entrance exam, and they diverted her into undercover assignments even before the academy."

"Shit," said Tanaka. "I didn't think they made that particular mistake anymore."

Coutinho knew what Tanaka meant. He had met the

first woman recruited to go undercover for the Honolulu police in the early 1980's. She had skipped the academy also, because her handlers didn't want anyone to know her as a cop.

He had an idea of the personal and professional price she had paid. Training and support were supposed to be better now.

"I guess they saw an opportunity to make a big case and felt they had to grab it. Hokoana must have done well enough, though."

"Or they wouldn't have sent her when we asked for somebody," said Tanaka. "That much makes sense. Where was this assignment?"

"She didn't exactly say, but she obviously knows Haleiwa inside and out."

"Then she knows how to handle herself."

The north shore of Oahu was the Wild West, with drugs and the surfers' vigilante code of conduct. The letter of the law was far down the list of priorities. Some of the cops who worked the district got so they fit right in.

"I guess."

Coutinho replayed the conversation in his mind.

"I didn't think much of it at the time, but she really didn't tell me anything. I'd ask her something, and she'd go off on something else, you know?"

"Her file says she's not married. Is there a boyfriend?"

"She didn't talk about that either."

"Here's the thing," said Tanaka. "You would expect her file to be thin, but not this thin."

"What did they give us here?"

Tanaka blew air out.

"Let's find out. Maybe we don't have to mention it to Internal Affairs."

"Ours or Honolulu?"

"Neither, if we're lucky. Start by questioning Hokoana's new boyfriend."

13

COUTINHO FOUND THE JOHN in Interview Two. He joined Kim in the adjoining room, where his partner was studying the man on the video monitor.

"He say anything?"

"Not a thing. No ID, either, but AFIS already gave us a hit. Kekili, Gabriel. From Waianae."

Waianae was possibly the toughest town on the island of Oahu.

"Matter of fact, Honolulu P.D. knows him very well."

Kim handed Coutinho a thick handful of printout pages.

"Busy boy," Coutinho said. "He's been smart or lucky."

Kekili had a long list of arrests for drug dealing and related offenses like assault and extortion, but no convictions since he had aged out of the juvenile justice system.

Prominent among the known associates was one Teddy Dias. Coutinho didn't know the name, but apparently it meant something on Oahu.

Could Kekili be the killer, in spite of the other man's confession? Coutinho thought back to the descriptions that various prostitutes had given of the man who had attacked them. They didn't match each other, and Kekili didn't match any of them. But Coutinho understood as well as anyone the unreliability of eyewitness testimony, especially under extreme stress. And a hooker might have her own agenda.

"He been stewing in there long enough?"

"Ready as he'll ever be. He's done this too many times to get a case of nerves."

"That just makes it more fun."

Kim didn't comment on his partner's bravado.

In the hall Coutinho stopped for a moment to prepare himself. As he thought of the questions he would ask, the door to Interview One opened, and a detective named Phillips came out.

"Hey, Coutinho. Solved your case for you."

"So I hear. What's he saying?"

"At the moment, not much. I think he regrets his moment of weakness."

"Do we have anything but his admission?"

"No problem. The knife was in the car, with obvious blood on it. Unless things really get weird and the blood doesn't match any of the victims, which I don't expect."

"Do we know him?"

"Take a look," said Phillips.

He opened the door again, long enough for Coutinho to take a look.

"Shit," said Coutinho. "Wally? What the hell is that about?"

Everybody knew Wally Watase. In Hilo a cop wasn't really a cop until he had brought Wally in for drunk and disorderly. Throwing a few punches was his style, and when he was drunk enough to get into a fighting mood, he took ten shots for every one he landed.

But hacking women up? It didn't figure at all.

"I know," said Phillips. "But the evidence doesn't lie."

"I guess not," said Coutinho.

But he hadn't convinced himself. Where had Wally been? The prostitute killer had been dormant for nine months and then burst out with a spasm of murderous violence. That wasn't an impossible interval for a serial killer, but it was on the long side. Usually it meant the man had been incapacitated, most often by a jail sentence.

Coutinho would have heard if Wally had done something to get himself more than a night in jail to sleep it off.

They would have to talk about that, but right now Wally had thrown him off. Coutinho had to start his mental preparations all over. When he felt ready, he entered the interview room. As he headed for the chair across the table from Kekili, he made a point of acting like a pompous bureaucrat. He studied the man's file, although he had already memorized the important information.

"So, Gabe. What brings you to Hilo?"

"I'm a tourist."

"Where you staying? The Hilo Hawaiian? That's where all the tourists go."

"With a buddy."

"Oh? Who do you know on the Big Island?"

"I forget his name."

"But he's a buddy."

"Right."

"He wouldn't be somebody who owes somebody on Oahu, would he?"

Kekili shrugged.

"How did you find the young lady?"

"Asked around. Some bartender."

"Paying for sex is illegal, Gabe. Anybody ever tell you that?"

"Well, you probably noticed, I didn't get laid, and I didn't have two hundred bucks on me, either."

"Good point. What you did have was a knife."

"It's part of my charm."

"You had something else in mind. What was it? A rip-off? Or do you just get off on killing hookers?"

Kekili looked smug.

"Or you were giving her a message. Who was the message from?"

"You still got nothing."

"Attempted murder is far from nothing."

"Okay, you got me carrying a knife."

"Also illegal, Gabe. You're just racking them up today."

Kekili didn't bother to reply.

"Here's the thing. You know and I know that no bartender told you about her. She advertises strictly online, and you don't strike me as a geek."

"Everybody lies to the cops. You gotta stop taking it personal."

Thanks to Hokoana, Coutinho had little to work with, and Kekili knew it. They went back and forth, until Coutinho felt that he could honorably withdraw from the room.

"Get comfortable, Gabe. Gonna be here a while."

He found Kim in the office they shared. It had probably started its career as a large-ish closet, because it was barely big enough for two desks.

"Did we record Hokoana and the moke, or were we just watching?"

"I got it. You could learn stuff like that, you know."

"That's why I put up with a fresh kid for a partner. Let's

watch it again."

Kim opened the laptop and pressed a button. Coutinho wondered why he wanted to watch again. Something must have bothered him the first time around, and now he had time to find out what it was. He concentrated on the moke's hands.

"There," he said and pointed at the screen. "He didn't have the knife in his hand, and he didn't take it out. She knocked it right out of his pocket."

The pockets of loose board shorts had a tendency to lose things when the wearer exerted himself.

"I see what you mean," said Kim.

"Now we have somebody else claiming to be the killer. And it looks like maybe Gabe didn't go in there planning to use that knife."

"So what's really going on?"

"Something else to ask Hokoana."

14

"FRIEND OF MINE is a Honolulu detective," said Tanaka. "He was willing to talk to me without asking too many questions. Which means I owe him."

Coutinho listened. This time Tanaka had found him and Kim in their office.

"He knows Jessie Hokoana from her undercover work. According to him, Hokoana's mother owns a Korean barbecue place in our territory. Waimea, matter of fact."

The capital of cattle country on the Big Island was a substantial drive north. Of course, everywhere on this island was a trip.

"He also told me that Jessie Hokoana has a half-brother on our turf. Younger. Turns out we know him too. Abie Noh."

"No shit. No wonder she didn't say anything."

It came up a lot. More than a few cops had relatives on the other side of the law, but they seldom broadcast it.

"Haven't heard much from him since the whole Schilling

thing," said Kim.

"Abie's still around," said Tanaka. "Guys like him never go away. If Hokoana wanted to hide on an island where she didn't know anybody else, she might go to him."

"Not her mother?" said Coutinho.

"According to my contact, that's not in the cards. Don't say I never did anything for you."

Tanaka turned and headed back toward his office. Coutinho and Kim sat looking at each other for a while.

"Josiah?" said Kim.

"It's a place to start."

"And if he can't help us?"

"We start looking for her."

"She could be anyplace on the island."

"Exactly."

"They call it the Big Island for a reason."

"Let's hope Josiah knows something."

The detectives left the station by the secure entrance. They climbed into Coutinho's car and headed toward the bay. They turned right on Kamehameha. Soon Ken's House of Pancakes appeared on their right. At ten-thirty in the morning the small parking lot was half full.

"Howzit, Connie," said Coutinho to the young blonde hostess in the blue flowered mu'u mu'u.

Connie had a tendency to wear nothing underneath, which gave Coutinho a tendency to stare that he worked to suppress.

"Is Josiah cooking?"

Connie looked displeased, but she nodded. The detectives went through the swinging door to the kitchen.

"Take five, Josiah," said Kim.

"For why you botha me?" said Josiah Kalama, all six-feet-two and one hundred and forty pounds of him. He cooked, but that didn't mean he ate. When he fell off the recovery wagon, meth was his nourishment, which was why he usually needed to earn points with the police.

"Ever seen her?" said Coutinho.

He held the picture of Hokoana under the cook's face.

"Why you need help finding a cop?" said Josiah.

So much for the effort of printing the screen capture. They might as well have used Hokoana's official file photo.

"Why would she be a cop?"

"Because I know all the girls been told by the cops to take a vacation. This young lady is trying to look like a hooker, but I know the hookers. *Quod erat demonstrandum*."

Josiah's education came out at odd moments. Sometimes very odd.

"Just let us know if you see her. Or if you hear about anybody who sounds like she might be this woman."

Josiah shrugged. "No promises."

"No, but you want us to like you."

"I get the message."

In the small parking lot attached to Ken's Coutinho and his partner sat for a moment before starting the car.

"Abie worked in Schilling's *pakalolo* operation."

A few years earlier the man who called himself Schilling had tried to monopolize the marijuana business on the Big Island. The experiment did not end well for Schilling.

"Schilling's dead. Left Abie short of gainful employment."

"So who picked up the slack in the *pakalolo* business?"

"That's easy. The same guy who took Schilling out. Morrison."

"Either Abie works for him now, or he knows what Abie is doing these days."

"Morrison will talk to us. Might not tell us much, but that's another matter."

15

THE DECISION LED to some down time, because a couple of detectives didn't just show up at a major drug dealer's front door. Coutinho and Kim waited in their office and tried to make a dent in the stacks of reports on their desks, while they waited for Tanaka's summons.

It came after only a couple of hours.

"You're good to go," said Tanaka. "Nobody's making a project of Morrison right now."

That meant the department's own drug investigators weren't keeping Morrison under surveillance, nor was any federal agency. There would be no eyebrows raised when two detectives called on the island's leading marijuana dealer.

Coutinho signed a Jeep out of the motor pool. Where he and Kim were going, all-wheel drive made good insurance.

He drove west on 11 and took 130 toward Pahoa. The route took him and his partner through scrub brush that was not what the Chamber of Commerce wanted tourists to see first. The Hawaiian homelands subdivisions, for residents with sufficient native Hawaiian ancestry, didn't look much more hopeful. Some of Coutinho's regular customers lived there.

He passed the turnoff to Pahoa, the major metropolis of the Puna district. Achieving that distinction didn't take much. The town had about three thousand residents.

The detectives took 130 to 132 and turned left. The highway made a typically abrupt island transition from bright sunlight to rainforest darkness. Except for college in Montana, Coutinho had lived his entire life on this island, but when he came to this part of Puna, he still felt like bringing his passport.

They made a couple of zigzag turns on nameless unpaved roads. The vehicle gave them jolt after merciless jolt, as the hard baked ruts refused to yield at all. Coutinho decided that he preferred mud to the moonscape that these roads became during a dry spell.

One moment the detectives were alone. The next a man stepped out of the forest and showed them his palm. He was a mostly Filipino bantamweight, but the Uzi in his other hand made up for his lack of bulk. Coutinho rolled his window down, and the fetid breath of the jungle crushed his air conditioning. In Puna, no rain didn't mean no humidity.

"I don't believe you're expected."

"We're not." Coutinho showed the man his shield. "Hide the gun. Now, before we take an interest in it."

The man put his gun hand into a pocket of his voluminous shorts. He gestured at Coutinho's shield.

"That don't change nothing. You're still not expected."

"It changes everything. Back up, or we put the cuffs on you. Maybe we keep you in the trunk until we're finished with your boss. Maybe forget about you until we get to Hilo."

The man stared for a moment to save face and then backed away.

Coutinho turned into the gap. He drove across the clearing that surrounded the house and parked right by the front door. The house was the usual one-story whitewashed box with a water tank on the roof and a generator grinding away out back.

The man they sought already stood in the doorway. Morrison hadn't lasted thirty years in his business by letting anyone sneak up on him.

Coutinho and Kim climbed out of their car. They kept their hands in view. Morrison knew that assassins could come in unexpected packaging, and he would have someone with a rifle watching the two detectives approach.

They stopped six feet from the man.

"Howzit, Coutinho."

Neither Coutinho nor Kim responded, but Morrison hadn't expected anything.

"Come in."

Morrison's main room had little furniture beyond some rolled up tatami mats. He led the detectives through the room to the kitchen, where a plain wooden table and four chairs awaited them. Morrison pointed toward two of the seats. Coutinho and Kim took two different chairs that allowed them to watch the door. It was their host's job to sit with his back to the doorway. If he couldn't trust the help, that was his problem.

"Abie Noh," said Coutinho.

"I know him."

"That's why we're here. Seen him lately?"

"I have a benefits program for my people," said Morrison.

"That's corporate of you."

"I'm serious. I give paid time off. Abie took some, starting this morning."

"Short notice."

"That's generally the way they need it. It wasn't a problem."

"Did he say why he needed time?"

"He has some family visiting."

"Did this ever come up before?"

"Now that you mention it, no. Not with Abie. I didn't know anything about his family."

"Who, exactly?"

"He didn't say."

"So he could have been lying."

"I suppose. But he's still entitled to the time. My feelings would be a little hurt, but I'd get over it."

"You got over him working for Schilling."

"Exactly. I took him back, no questions asked. I'm easy to get along with."

"Okay, the big question. Where did Abie go?"

"I don't know. Hitting the highlights, maybe. This relative must be from off-island."

"Right. Four days and three nights in the Kohala resorts."

Coutinho's mind made a leap. He wasn't quite sure how he knew where Jessie Hokoana was, but he knew.

"Who's at Schilling's place these days?"

"Nobody that I know of."

"Come on. A house free and clear, no taxes, no bills, no paper trail? Somebody took it over."

Much of the land in Puna had no certain ownership, thanks to a century of confusion at the Bishop estate, the largest landowner in the state. Many local people took advantage of the situation by squatting on the land. Entire neighborhoods thrived where tax and utility maps showed undeveloped land.

"Seems to us," said Kim, "that you would want to protect

your flank and not let anybody move into Schilling's place."

"If we go there," said Coutinho, "are we going to find Abie and his sister?"

"I couldn't tell you."

"Okay, play it that way. But if we find out you called them, you're going to have a real problem with us. I know you don't have much experience with cop problems. You keep things calm, you don't get too big or embarrass us, so we concentrate on people who don't know the rules. You could end up changing that."

"Like I said, I'm easy to get along with."

16

THE WOMAN DROPPED JESSIE OFF at the pancake house.

"You sure you're okay?"

"Yeah," said Jessie. "I'm good. As long as I get here before my husband, he won't ask any questions. Thanks for the help."

The middle-aged Hawaiian woman nodded without conviction and drove off. Jessie paused for a moment to let her conflicting emotions settle. The woman had a good heart, and Jessie wasn't pleased with herself for exploiting it. On the other hand, her story about a clandestine shopping expedition with a girlfriend her husband didn't like, and then an argument with the girlfriend, who retaliated by stranding Jessie downtown, all confirmed that her undercover instincts still worked. That was gratifying. So did choosing the woman in the first place. Out of all the people milling around Hilo's downtown, Jessie had recognized the one who would help.

She turned away from the busy intersection and went into the restaurant. The waiting area was still retro enough to have a pay phone, which she had noticed her first time in the place. She dropped coins and punched numbers.

The fifth ring gave her a bad moment. She couldn't leave a voicemail message, because she couldn't trust it to end up in the right hands. But then a youthful-sounding male voice said, "What?"

"Did Mom teach you to answer a phone like that?"

"Who's this?"

"Jessie."

Silence.

"Your sister Jessie, Abie. I'm here on the island."

"How'd you get this number?"

He sounded surly, but she made allowances. Drug dealers didn't like their phone numbers getting out.

"Mom gave it to me a while back."

Abie's silence said he didn't like that, either, but second-guessing his mother was not an option.

"What do you need?"

"A ride, for starters."

"Why?"

"Just trust me on this, Abie."

That was asking a lot. They had a blood relationship but little shared history beyond a few awkward childhood encounters.

"You're a cop."

"Not just a cop, Abie. *Ohana*."

There. She had said it. The word meant family, and there was no more important concept in Hawaii. Family meant a web of obligations, some explicit, others expressed in nods, shrugs, and lowered voices in the night.

"Twenty minutes," Abie said. "Better get coffee or

71

something inside."

He had a point. She was too conspicuous loitering where she was. She went from the vestibule to the hostess station and pointed a finger at the counter. The young woman in the mu'u mu'u was multi-tasking too hard to do more than nod.

And equally harried waitress set down a cup and waited with the carafe. Jessie nodded, and the waitress poured the first cup. Jessie looked up and noticed a gaunt cook in the open kitchen. He gave her a look that left no doubt in her mind. He would remember her.

Or was that just undercover adrenaline making her see things?

Wherever Abie was when she called him, he had his timing down. Twenty-two minutes elapsed on her watch, before a lean young man with spiky hair and ropey fore-arms sidled into the restaurant as if he wanted to present the smallest possible target.

The sight of him summoned more memories than she had expected, of a bratty, uncontrollable younger boy. Now he looked like someone she might have to pat down and cuff.

He recognized her also. She dropped three singles on the counter and slid off the stool onto the floor. He turned and left the restaurant. It was up to her whether she followed.

He also let her handle the passenger door herself. Jessie suppressed a grimace at the grime-encrusted Jeep Wrangler.

That was another thing. How did people on this island keep their RAVs and Wranglers straight? Maybe they didn't. Maybe they treated the vehicles like public bicycles in Amsterdam.

Jessie told herself to get a grip. She put her seatbelt on, but Abie didn't bother with his. That didn't surprise her. Under the circumstances she decided to ignore her cop reflexes and say nothing.

"You're in some deep shit, is all I can figure," said Abie.

"You're not wrong about that."

"Do I want to know?"

"Let's just say I had a situation. They told me I would be safe as long as I got off Oahu. Turns out they were wrong. I'm not even sure I can trust the local cops."

"But you trust me."

"*Ohana*."

She had said it again, and it might be one time too many.

"You don't have to tell me. Just so you know, I ain't stupid. You're a cop. Mom says you been out of touch for a long time. To me that says undercover. They wouldn't send you after Morrison, because I'd spot you, and that would be that."

That was some pretty sophisticated reasoning from the boy she remembered.

"And if it ain't my boss you're after, I don't care who it is."

Jessie nodded.

"One thing, though," said Abie. "You might want to tell me who's gonna come after us. So I can spot them coming."

"Only thing I can tell you, they won't be anybody you know. They'll be from off-island."

"Doesn't narrow it down much."

Abie turned left onto another mud road, hardened in the drought. Like many of the roads in Puna, it lacked a sign or visible markings, and it probably wouldn't appear on any map of the island. Jessie wondered how Abie could tell where he was. This was a different world from the Kona side of the island, where the tourists went for sun and surf.

Not that she liked Kona. Not anymore. She didn't like any place where climate reminded her too much of Mexico. That was a memory too recent and too overpowering for her to process yet.

"Where are we going?" she said.

"Someplace nobody will find us."

"You sure?"

"Sure as I can be. The place belonged to a guy I used to work for. Nobody there now."

She had no choice about trusting him. She just wished that it came more easily.

"You know," said Abie, "this is a little weird. Being the man of the family, I mean."

Jessie fought the impulse to tell him he was wrong. It wasn't the time.

"Your father is gone, and so is mine."

Now he was really making it difficult.

Abie turned and gave her long look. There was no other traffic, but the jungle crowded the road on both sides. There was plenty to hit if their wheels strayed.

"Abie, watch the road."

He did for a while.

"What do you remember about your father?" he said.

There he was, looking at her again.

"The road."

"I just want to know," he said with his eyes forward.

"I'm guessing Mom didn't talk much about him."

"She dropped a few hints. I found people to fill in some blanks. Turns out he was a legend."

"What kind of people?"

"The kind of people who aren't afraid of anybody. But they were afraid of him."

"I don't remember being afraid of him. Ever."

"I think you're the only one."

He wrenched the wheel to the right, and for a moment Jessie thought he wanted to kill them both. But the Jeep slipped through a barely visible gap in the ferns and bamboo.

"We're here."

17

COUTINHO REMEMBERED Schilling's old place. It was just a few loops and turns away from Morrison's house, but it meant twenty minutes of slogging in the mud or bouncing on hard ruts. He thought back to the time when it had been war between the two dealers, but it felt like several lifetimes ago. He still had to stay alert for the gap in the jungle that would be his only landmark. He slowed and turned in.

He saw that he had guessed right. Morrison had been keeping the place up. It was his way of telling the local residents that the house wasn't available. The jungle still kept its distance around the house—not a respectful distance, but the rainforest respected nothing. Someone had cranked the window slats open in the dry weather, which meant that someone was available to close them when it rained.

Coutinho looked at the house and knew at once that something was wrong. The door flapped open in a way that seemed to call for help. He glanced at Kim, who already had his gun out. They separated and crossed the clearing to opposite corners of the building. It was a small clearing that left Coutinho exposed for just a few seconds, but that was more than long enough to make him feel like a target. He paused to get a breath and watched Kim do the same. They didn't need words. Their only choice was to duck under the windows, pivot, and pile through the doorway. They couldn't wait for backup, not when someone might be dying on the floor.

Kim went first. He was younger, faster and lighter, and he would spend a fraction of a second less framed in the doorway. Coutinho followed. They made it inside without drawing fire. Kim cut to the left and Coutinho to the right.

They cleared the four rooms quickly. In the bedroom they found a young man bound and gagged on the bed.

No one else was in the house.

Coutinho went outside. He made a circuit around the house, but it didn't do much good. The clearing was deserted, but a battalion of Marines could be lurking in the jungle, and he would never know. All he had was a gut feeling that no one was around.

He went back inside.

"Abie. You don't look so good."

The young man glared as Kim worked the gag loose.

"What happened?" said Coutinho.

"He got her," Abie said. "Couldn't do a damn thing."

"Who?'

"King fucking Kamehameha."

"What are you talking about, Abie?"

"Hawaiian guy. Huge, but not the way they usually are."

"What's that mean?"

"Muscles on top of muscles. Like I said, fucking Kamehameha. Twice my age, twice my size. Handled me like a four-year-old."

"He took Jessie?"

"I guess. I heard them talking first, but I couldn't hear much of it. From the sound of it, she was walking. He didn't have to carry her."

"Did you catch anything of what they said?"

"Yeah. Something about a *pu'uhonua*."

A place of refuge in the traditional Hawaiian religion.

"We're going to untie you," said Coutinho. "If you behave, that is. You going to behave?"

"Yeah."

Again Kim did the honors.

"You want to get checked out, Abie?"

"Nah. He didn't hit me or nothing. Didn't have to."

Coutinho studied the young man. Okay, he was humiliated over losing a fight, but something more than that was eating at him.

"Did you know the moke, Abie?"

"No."

"But you know who he is."

Abie stared stoically into the distance, which Coutinho took as an admission.

"Abie, I know your file. You've told us a lot of bullshit."

"Sometimes it's even the truth."

Abie was digging in and getting ready to be interrogated. He had plenty of experience, and Coutinho knew he didn't have the time to break the young man down.

"Okay. Wait downstairs for us. And I mean wait, or you'll have to walk to Hilo."

"I get the message."

Abie tottered a little as he left, as if the blood hadn't returned to his extremities, but he was young enough to recover quickly.

Coutinho looked at his partner

"King Kamehameha gets traditional religion."

"There's a lot of that going around," said Kim.

"And Jessie wasn't fighting back."

"Sounds like she knew him."

"She probably met a lot of people when she was under-cover. Maybe that was one of them."

"We need to find out."

18

"IF I DIDN'T KNOW BETTER," said Morrison. "I'd say it sounds like Hosea Hokoana. That's a name I haven't heard for a while."

Coutinho glanced at his partner and then back at Morrison.

"You got here, when?" said Coutinho.

"Thirty years ago. More than thirty."

That put his arrival in the early to mid-nineteen-seventies.

"So how did you know Hosea Hokoana?"

"He came from Ni'ihau, was what I heard. But what I know for sure is, he made it hard to do business. All my guys were scared to death of him. Hosea was hiring out as muscle, and a lot of businessmen caught on that they were a step ahead just bringing him to a meet."

"How did you handle that?"

"I put my foot down, finally. I spread the word that I wouldn't meet with anyone if they brought Hosea. And if I saw him, I would walk."

"Did that solve the problem?"

"Not so you'd notice. He started going outlaw on the outlaws—sticking up businessmen."

"You can say dealer, Morrison. We know what you mean, and right now we don't care."

"I don't want to pick up any bad habits."

"So what happened to him? Did he go to jail?"

"All these years, I thought he was dead."

"Why would you think that?"

"He pissed off the wrong people."

"Who would that have been back then?"

"Try Satan's Right Hand."

"The bikers? No shit."

"They were trying to move in on the island. I heard he robbed one of them. Bad career move."

"How did that it out?"

"Nobody knew the details, but Hosea disappeared right about that time. Which is why I figured he was dead."

"You ever meet any of the bikers?"

"Hell yes. They summoned me to a meeting. Told me I could retire or I could go hard, but I was going."

"So who was at this meeting?"

"Couple of tons worth of bikers. Bear in mind that I've been here for thirty years. I've seen a lot of Hawaiians. Not just Hosea. And I'm telling you, I never saw so many huge men."

He grimaced.

"I guess nobody made bathtubs in their size. I can still smell them."

"So SRH wanted you out, but that's not how it turned out. What got in their way?"

"How come you don't know your history?"

It was a bit of a taunt, and Coutinho gave Morrison a sample of his flat-eyed cop look. Morrison knew that the Hawaii County Police had some dubious history if you went back a few years. The Feds had often cut them out of investigations.

Morrison shrugged an apology.

"The Feds came in and rolled them up all at once. The biggest case they ever made on this island, and SRH never got started."

"Who's still around from that time?" said Coutinho.

"Me."

"That's what I'm thinking."

Coutinho gave Morrison a little more of his cop stare.

"Funny how you knew who we were talking about right away. I think maybe you're not just talking about ancient history. Like maybe Hosea Hokoana just showed up and refreshed your memory. You wouldn't have warned him about us just to get him to go away? Or told him where to find Jessie and Abie?"

Morrison didn't flinch.

"Wait until you meet him. Tell me you wouldn't do a lot to make him somebody else's problem. Just speaking hypothetically."

"Did he say why he's back after all this time?"

"Hosea never did much explaining. He didn't have to."

19

"THAT WAS MEAN TO ABIE," Jessie said.

Her father was driving another Excursion. She was concluding that he intended to ignore her, when he said, "He's young. He'll get over it."

For some reason that irked her. She decided that thinking aloud would help her figure out why.

"I don't know about that. I don't think you understand how much crap most people have to swallow in a lifetime. We don't need any more. Abie definitely didn't."

She expected him to say something along the lines of, "That's their problem," but he surprised her.

"You're probably right. I don't have much experience with that."

She glanced at him again. How many people on the planet could make him hold still for a reprimand like that? She might be the only one.

"Abie could help us. He knows people."

"And people know him. Not a good thing if you want to go underground."

"Undercover to underground," Jessie said. "Not a good trend. Makes me wonder what's next."

"You're with me now."

"Does that mean we're going anywhere in particular?"

They were on another narrow dirt road. The rainforest still looked featureless to her. Tree branches, ferns, impossibly long grasses grabbed the huge Excursion from both sides, from above, and even from below.

"I have a place set up. Not far."

Without warning the road dumped them out of the forest onto a paved highway. Her father turned right and gave the vehicle gas. They began passing evenly spaced side roads lined with small, boxy houses. Jessie knew a Hawaiian homelands subdivision when she saw one.

Hosea turned left and drove for about five minutes. They passed a bank of mailboxes and then arrived at a very different kind of place, a community of houses on stilts. There was only the one road into the subdivision, and the buildings were tightly packed. He drove straight through to the last row of houses, which perched on the edge of the ocean.

Jessie felt a smile, her first in weeks, spread across her face. As a child, she would have squealed with delight. These houses didn't have back yards. They had tide pools. She could imagine jumping from the kitchen straight into the ocean.

But her smile disappeared as quickly as it had come.

"What is this place?"

"Kapoho tide pools."

"Is it safe? Lots of eyes around."

"We won't stick out. A lot of these houses are short term rentals. New people coming and going all the time. Only place like it on the Hilo side."

Most visitors went to the sunny Kona side of the island.

"So, we should be okay here for a while. At least until that thing I told you about comes up."

"Hiding in plain sight," said Jessie. "I like it."

20

"CATTLE COUNTRY," said Coutinho.

He and Kim had just left Honoka'a behind. The highway veered westward toward the town of Waimea. Beef cattle lined up at the wire fences along the highway and regarded the passing traffic with solemnity, or maybe stupidity. It was hard to tell.

"I always feel weird up here," said Kim. "Like it's Wyoming or something."

"You ever been to Wyoming?"

"Waimea, Wyoming. Close enough."

"You're not wrong," said Coutinho. "I went to college in Montana. Got down to Wyoming a couple of times. Rodeos and stuff. I figured, when in Rome."

He snorted a humorless laugh.

"Got into a fight with a cowboy in Sheridan."

"What was his problem?"

"I never found out. Maybe I look like a Democrat."

"How did that go?"

"The way it usually does. I said I won, he said he did."

They passed the agricultural coop and started to see roadside businesses.

"There's the place," said Coutinho.

Noh's Korean Barbecue was second from the right in a six-storefront strip mall. Coutinho signaled a left turn and pulled into the parking lot. Kim gave the place a contemptuous look.

"What?" said Coutinho.

"Lately you can't throw a stick without hitting a Korean barbecue joint. What makes a *haole wahine* think she can cut it?"

"You heard what Tanaka said. White woman or not, it's supposed to be good."

They got out of the car.

"What the hell," said Kim. "Maybe so. It's not like these places are the real thing. Not when you had a grandmother from the old country."

"Good enough for me."

"My point exactly."

"You saying I don't know how to eat? Nobody beats a Portuguese grandmother for da *ono* kind grinds."

Still bickering, they pulled the door open. The lunch rush was probably over, which was good. There was no point in annoying a witness before they even started asking questions.

That had to be Hilly Noh behind the counter. She looked like any white woman who had spent her whole life in the subtropical sun. Whatever her natural coloring, she was a blonde now, with mahogany skin.

But the coloring that made many women resemble beef jerky made her look hot. Coutinho had an eye mostly for women around his own age. He considered that nothing more than good sense. But Hilly Noh had something going that made her age irrelevant. Discerning young men would also go for her.

Coutinho had his detective ID ready.

"Mrs. Noh?"

She didn't look pleased. She also made a point of scrutinizing his credential.

"What did Abie do this time?"

"It's not about Abie."

She looked puzzled.

"This is Detective Kim, by the way."

She nodded without enthusiasm. "What can I do for you?"

"It's about your husband."

"What could you want with him? He's gone almost ten years now. And he would rather chew his own arm off than break the law."

"Your first husband."

"Now that," she said, "is not my favorite topic."

But she turned and fired a string of words at a tiny Korean woman in her sixties. It took Coutinho a moment to realize that she hadn't spoken English. Hilly Noh turned back to the detectives and continued in the same language. Kim shook his head.

"I'm third generation. Never learned Korean."

"Sorry. Didn't mean to put you on the spot. After all these years, I see a Korean-looking face and out it comes."

"Never heard it from anyone who wasn't Korean," said Kim.

"You want to learn a language, run a restaurant for twenty years."

She led them to one of the half dozen tables. Like many such places, the restaurant did mostly takeout.

"Sit. Okay, why should I care about Hosea Hokoana at this late date?"

"We think he's around."

"That's pretty bad news."

"For you?"

"For anybody."

Unlike Morrison, the woman seemed genuinely surprised. He didn't think Hosea Hokoana had come to his ex-wife. Not yet, anyway.

"Was he abusive?"

"Not to me. I'm about the only person he ever knew that he didn't end up beating the crap out of. Me and Jessie. My daughter. His, too."

"Would Jessie know if he was back?"

"Couldn't tell you."

"When did you talk to her last?"

"Hard to say."

"You don't get along?"

"She lives on a different island."

"She's here right now."

"News to me."

Hilly Noh met Coutinho's cop look better than a lot of mokes would have done.

"She's got her career. No time for *ohana*."

In a disapproving tone she came out with several phrases in what Coutinho recognized as Hawaiian. It sounded fluent.

"I guess you learned Hawaiian from Hosea."

"Not just him. I grew up on Kauai, knew kids from Ni'ihau who came over for preschool. I didn't even know it was Hawaiian I was speaking."

"So Hosea had to leave Ni'ihau when he married you."

"I think that's why he married me. To get off that island. Couldn't wait. Then he did a complete one-eighty."

"How do you mean?"

"Couldn't get along with the *haole* at all. Got fired from a few jobs. Wore out his welcome on Kauai, and we ended up here."

"More elbow room," said Coutinho to encourage her.

"That was when he started getting militant. The old religion, traditional canoeing, hula. And traditional food. He grew up on Spam. All of a sudden he's eating fish and poi."

"Sounds like a good way to get into shape."

"Tell me about it. Way over three hundred pounds, all of it muscle. And attitude."

She was leading to the obvious conclusion, but she seemed to be waiting for Coutinho to say it. He obliged.

"He had to make a living somehow. *Pakalolo?* Meth? Enforcement?"

"All of the above."

"He had no arrest record."

"Everybody was scared to death of him. Nobody complained to the cops."

"But I think you're saying he loved Jessie."

"He could sit there for hours holding her. Only time he ever reminded me of what I first saw in him."

"But he left her. And you."

"Had to. He finally pissed off somebody he couldn't just punch out. Damn, this is a long time ago."

"Who was that?"

She waved a hand.

"Gang stuff."

"You don't know who?"

"I made a point of not knowing. I'm not proud of it, but we had bills, and he brought home the cash."

"Where did he go?"

"I heard rumors about Mexico."

"Did Jessie know that?"

"I couldn't say."

Again she met his eyes, but a little conviction had leaked out of her tone.

"But you never heard anything from him."

"Not a word. I divorced him for abandonment."

"So he's alive?"

"No idea."

21

COUTINHO WANTED PANCAKES, and he wanted them bad. He looked at his watch and saw that he had time.

He went to Ken's House of Pancakes. That much was a no-brainer. In Ken's they served everything with pancakes, even if you begged them not to give you any.

"Howzit, Connie?"

"Howzit, Coutinho."

Connie was still a little cool to him after the other day.

"I'm just here to eat, Connie. Not for botha Josiah."

He took a seat at the counter and ordered island-style corned beef hash and eggs. He drank coffee and tried to convince himself that Lucy wouldn't come through the door and give him that look.

Her special, proprietary Who Said You Could Eat That look.

He reminded himself that she was on a different island, but he still couldn't get used to the idea. He told himself that she was his ex-wife now, and he could eat what he wanted, but he didn't believe that, either.

On top of it all, he had a weird feeling. Somebody was watching him. He might wish it was Lucy, but it couldn't be. He started scanning the room.

The answer was right in front of him. In the kitchen Josiah set two dishes on the pass-through under the warming lamps. The waitress took them and delivered them to Coutinho. Josiah stayed where he was. He was looking distinctly exasperated, and Coutinho realized that it was the cook who had beaming telepathic rays at him.

Josiah looked around and then flashed five fingers. Coutinho shook his head and flashed five fingers three times. Even fifteen minutes weren't enough to savor hash, eggs and pancakes, but Josiah looked antsy, as if he had something important to say. His judgment was usually good.

Of course, the secret agent nonsense was futile. The right side of Coutinho's face started burning, and he knew the cause. Connie's scathing look was almost as good as Lucy's.

He stretched the fifteen minutes to twenty and then took his check to Connie, who took it and his twenty without a word.

"Sorry, Connie, I'll make it quick."

He detoured back to lay a couple of singles on the counter and then went out and around to the rear of the restaurant. Josiah waited.

"I hear you're looking for somebody."

"We told you that."

"Two somebodies. The young lady, and a very large gentleman. I know where they're gonna be."

Josiah explained. It sounded like good information. Worth passing up the rest of the coffee in the carafe, because Connie would already have retaliated by clearing it away.

22

"THE VOLCANOES?" said Tanaka. "What for?"

Tanaka left Coutinho and Kim standing in front of his desk.

"Hosea Hokoana, we think. And Jessie."

"You think?"

"Josiah heard about a major ritual off Chain of Craters Road. Supposed to last all night."

Coutinho had meant to keep it vague about some confidential informant, but Tanaka's expression said he wouldn't have bought it.

"A lot of people are into that. Doesn't have to involve Hokoana."

"This thing does. The way Josiah described it, it's big. If Hokoana is on the island, that's where we'll find him."

Tanaka blew air out.

"It's a religious observance. Tread lightly. Relations with the community would never recover."

"We'll be outnumbered. We'll have to mind our manners."

"And you think our Hokoana is with him."

"Looks like it. We have it from Hosea's ex-wife that his daughter meant a lot to him. And if Abie's right, she went with him voluntarily."

Tanaka waved them out of his office. Coutinho and Kim stopped in the hallway.

"I guess we go to Chain of Craters."

"But quietly. We can forget about backup."

"I have an idea," said Coutinho. "We have to notify her anyway, because it's her territory."

He looked sideways at Kim.

"And I know what that grin is about."

23

COUTINHO PUNCHED THE NUMBERS into his phone. He detected no butterflies in his stomach, which surprised him.

It turned out that his nerves were just toying with him. The first ring made his pulse accelerate. The second turned his breathing shallow. Lucy's "Hello" before the third ring summoned such a vivid mental picture of her that Coutinho couldn't speak.

Forty-two, he thought.

Her age. His ex-wife was the kind of blonde who came into her own after forty, and he was missing it.

He looked across the kitchen table at her customary seat. Even the late afternoon sunlight seemed to miss her. He had never seen her new apartment in Honolulu, and he didn't want to.

"Hello?" she said again.

Her caller ID must have told her who was interrupting her evening, but she was going to make him work for it.

"It's Errol," he was able to croak this time.

Now she was the one making the silence. This threatened to be a very awkward conversation.

"How are you, Errol?"

"Fine. How's life in the big city?"

"I thought that was Pahoa."

It had once been their private joke. The first time Coutinho took Lucy to Pahoa to show her the psychedelic murals on the buildings and the sixties' people on the wooden side-walks, he had called it "the big city." When she got the joke, he knew she was a keeper.

A keeper he hadn't managed to keep.

"Honolulu's a little overwhelming," she said. "But I can't beat the commute."

She lived just blocks away from the crime lab, where she worked as a DNA analyst. Coutinho was glad she couldn't see him wince. He couldn't leave the Big Island; she couldn't stay there. They were at an impasse.

"Got a date," he said.

The comment started as a joke, but somehow it emerged with more bite than he intended.

"Glad to hear it," she said after a pause, and he understood. She was the one who was dating, and the cop grapevine had told him who the lucky man was.

"It's about work," he said too quickly. "Ann Wessel. You remember her?"

"I remember any woman who makes me feel that inadequate."

"Don't say that, Luce. On a scale of one to Lucy, she's a… six."

He waited to hear where she would go with that opening, but she dropped it.

"You have a case taking you to the park?"

"Yeah," he said. "Not drugs, though."

Now he kicked himself for bringing it up. She would still fear the worst. She wouldn't believe that he wasn't taking on the marijuana farmers or meth cookers who operated clandestinely on national park land, and protected their turf with military-grade weapons.

"Really. We just need Ann for jurisdiction."

"Be careful. I only have one ex-husband."

"You'll still have one. Promise."

24

COUTINHO PICKED KIM UP at his apartment at two in the morning.

"Get any sleep?"

They still had the rest of the night and a long day ahead of them.

"Didn't even try," Kim said. He looked stoic about it.

Coutinho had done four hours in the rack. It was one of the dubious benefits of middle age. For years he had been waking up in the small hours of every night. Half the time he couldn't nod off again. This morning he had something better to do than lie there staring at the ceiling.

He drove his own Camry. During the long climb up Highway 11 to the entrance of Volcanoes National Park Kim snored a little. He would deny that he had dozed, and under the circumstances Coutinho would let him get away with it.

Ann Wessel waited for them at the visitors' center. Coutinho climbed out and shook her hand. Kim did the same. He looked fully awake. Wessel had that effect on most men.

She was an inch or two taller than either of them. Her strong cheekbones and stronger nose went well with her height and athletic build. Nature had given her a face that looked intriguing when it was tanned and weather-beaten, and the sun had done a better job of streaking her dark blond hair than a three-hundred-dollar salon.

Coutinho suspected that she had her law enforcement ranger uniforms tailored. He appreciated the effort.

He filled her in beyond what he had told her on the phone the day before.

"You understand," she said, "we can't just go barging in. It's *kapu* for non-Hawaiians. We could make a noise that would carry all the way to Washington."

"We're not going to intrude, Ann. We just need to be there when things break up. We'll wait."

"Just remember, it's at least my job if we fuck it up. Yours too, probably."

She led them to a Park Service jeep and put her right foot down hard. She had them going more than twenty miles an hour before Coutinho had settled himself in his seat.

In minutes they had left the visitors center and the lodge behind, and the only illumination was their own headlights. This side of the island was usually overcast at night, and tonight was no exception. Coutinho could see nothing but the road directly ahead of them, but he knew that off to his right was the huge Kilauea crater. Fortunately for him and the visitors sleeping in the lodge, Kilauea wasn't in the active volcanic zone.

Unless the goddess Pele got up on the wrong side of the bed and decided to shake things up.

After a while they had circled enough of the crater to see

the lights from the inhabited area where they had started. The whole residential complex looked like a child's model. A little further on, trees and other vegetation intervened.

Coutinho wasn't ready for it when Wessel veered off the road and stopped on the shoulder. He swayed against her, which wasn't unpleasant. She turned the headlights off, and then the engine.

"We have a little time. I want you to see this."

"What?" said Kim. "It's too dark to see anything."

"Exactly. Darkness. Real darkness. You have any idea how rare that is?"

They sat in silence for a good five minutes, until Wessel started the engine and put the vehicle in drive. The headlights came on.

"You see that, and you start to understand all the myths and supernatural stories of pre-modern peoples. We sit in our living rooms with our electric lights, and it's easy to laugh. Imagine half of the planet in that kind of darkness. You'd go a little crazy too."

Coutinho thought she had a point.

"Sorry." Wessel snorted with laughter that seemed directed at herself. "Maybe I'm the one who's crazy."

"No," said Kim. "That makes sense."

He seemed to mean it beyond wanting to get into Wessel's pants.

They reached the turnoff for the Chain of Craters Road.

"I've never been down here," said Kim.

He sounded a little embarrassed.

"Really?" said Wessel. "Then you buy the gas. It's a park tradition."

"Come on. I know that much."

Wessel laughed.

"We get people who don't. We have to deliver emergency

gas all the time. No matter how many times people hear it, they can't believe there's nothing from here on."

Coutinho had done the drive before. He knew that nothing meant nothing—no convenience stores, no gas stations, no water fountains, no street lights, nothing but flat black volcanic rock. In only twenty winding miles the road descended three thousand feet to sea level.

Three times during the trip they met headlights coming up the mountain. Hardcore lava fans liked to spend the night at the observation point at the end of the road. They wouldn't be going quite that far.

Dawn began to soften the darkness. They negotiated a switchback and saw a cluster of vehicles parked beside the highway. Most were battered Jeeps or aging Toyota RAVs. Other than the vehicles, Coutinho could see no obvious landmark.

"That's them," Wessel said.

She parked behind a RAV.

"I hope they're in a good mood."

From this distance there was no way to tell, especially not in the half light, but Coutinho could see a couple of dozen people, men and women in roughly equal numbers. They looked Hawaiian.

Twenty minutes later, in another abrupt island transition, the daylight had become complete. The group of Hawaiians broke up into twos and threes and began to return to their vehicles. One of the women was Jessie Hokoana. Walking with her ahead of the others in the group was a man Coutinho had never met but recognized anyway.

King Fucking Kamehameha, Abie Noh had said.

He looked closer to four hundred pounds than three, and all of it was muscle. Make that muscle and scars, at least one on his shirtless torso for each of his roughly fifty years.

Coutinho saw no gun, but that didn't reassure him. This man wouldn't need one.

"You're not welcome here," said the man as he came into speaking range.

"You would be Hosea Hokoana," said Coutinho.

"That doesn't matter."

The huge man's mouth twitched. Coutinho didn't know what could be funny about a visit from the police, but someone like Hokoana probably looked at things differently.

"You're not one of us. For you this isn't *pu'uhonua.*"

Pu'uhonua. A place of refuge in the traditional Hawaiian religion. Someone who looked directly at a chief or cast a shadow across his would receive a death sentence. The offender could then try to outrun pursuit to a designated place where a priest could perform rituals to lift the sentence.

"We haven't violated *kapu,*" said Wessel. "This is a public highway."

"We don't recognize your jurisdiction."

"Daddy," said a female voice. "This isn't the time."

"It's *kapu,* Jessie," said her father.

He continued in a language that Coutinho almost didn't recognize. He didn't speak Hawaiian, but now it was being used to decide his fate.

It was appropriate if he took the long view, say, back to Cook's arrival in 1778 or the American coup of 1893, but Coutinho didn't have time for history lessons.

Jessie answered in Hawaiian. The discussion got heated, and Jessie switched to English.

"It's not *pu'uhonoa* yet. The *kahuna* hasn't performed the rituals. If we punish them, we're *kapu.*"

Something forbidden, or the person who had done the forbidden thing. *Kahuna.* Priest. Coutinho knew the terms. Everyone who had gone to school in Hawaii knew them, but they sounded different now.

"They've seen our place," said Hosea. "They'll be back with more cops."

Wessel had the sense to let Jessie keep handling it.

"Daddy, you said yourself. The old religion has to make itself new for the modern world."

Hosea looked at them without expression. Coutinho knew beyond doubt that the man had killed before. The novelty had worn off, and so had any hesitation.

"You're lucky my daughter is here. Turn around and go."

Coutinho shook his head.

"We need to take Jessie with us. She's a police officer, and it's her duty to come."

"You're pressing your luck."

"Doing our job, we call it."

Hosea stood for a moment, massive and motionless.

"Enough talk. Time for you to go."

"If you don't let us take her, you can come with us in handcuffs."

"Put them on me."

Coutinho had to admit that the man's confidence was justified.

"You know we can't let this go. Somebody could get killed, and it doesn't have to happen."

Coutinho knew to the millimeter where his right hand was in relation to his gun. The clarity was strange, because the hand seemed to belong to someone else, someone almost as cool under fire as Hosea Hokoana. The hand didn't tremble or stray toward the weapon. Through his eerie calm Coutinho wondered when he would start feeling concerned. A man the size of Hosea Hokoana could take an entire clip in the body and still do a lot of damage.

Then it occurred to Coutinho to ask himself what he was

doing face down in the gap between two boulders embedded in the hard ground. He decided that wedging himself in even deeper wouldn't be a bad idea. To his right Kim and Ann Wessel were also digging for cover. The crack of the gunshot that had sent them all sprawling became a memory before Coutinho recognized it for what it was.

But more shots followed, too many to count. Training and experience took over. His nine-millimeter appeared in his right hand. He didn't know where the sniper was, but instinct told him that uphill was the obvious choice. The shooter would want an escape route. Coutinho fired three rounds, starting from the left and working to his right. He glanced back for a moment. Kim was on top of Ann Wessel, shielding her as he fired.

It was futile. The shots sounded like a rifle. If the sniper had any brains at all, he was out of pistol range.

The Hawaiians were also trying to hide behind rocks or vehicles or anything else that offered cover. Glass shattered, as a rifle bullet met a windshield. A tire popped, and one of the Jeeps listed to the side.

Hosea Hokoana wasn't where Coutinho had last seen him. He had dropped and rolled six feet to his right, where he could take cover beside a Ford Excursion. It was the only vehicle that was big enough for him, so it must be his.

"I would appreciate it," Hokoana said, "if you gentlemen with the guns would keep firing."

Coutinho had never heard such calm in a situation like this one.

"What will that do?"

Now he was doing it too—conversing as if they were sitting over coffee at Ken's.

"I have a rifle in my vehicle. I need to get it."

"That's a plan."

Coutinho and Kim nodded at each other. On a count of three they pushed themselves to their feet and ran in a crouch toward Ann Wessel's Jeep, which was in a good position to provide some cover. Their movement drew two more rifle shots, which skittered off the rocks with a sound like a lethal rain shower.

The sniper paused. He had fired enough rounds that he might need a new magazine. The two detectives both popped up and started pulling their triggers. They couldn't hope for accuracy. They could only try to intimidate the shooter with rapid fire. Hosea would have to get to his rifle fast, because they would run out of ammunition soon.

Coutinho glanced over at the Excursion. Hosea had the rear driver's side door open and had raised himself off the ground to reach inside the vehicle.

Two shots came. The first shattered the Excursion's window on the uphill side. The second followed the path of the first and struck Jessie Hokoana with a vicious thud. She rolled over on her back and seemed to look up at the overcast sky with mild surprise.

Coutinho could see the star-shaped hole in her forehead. He held his position behind the Jeep, but silence returned.

The sniper had accomplished what he had come to do.

25

COUTINHO LOOKED AROUND for help that he didn't expect. The civilians were useless. They were still trying to figure out what had happened.

He counted to ten and stood. Nothing but silence came from the shooter's direction. Kim climbed to his feet and joined him in looking uphill.

"Did you see where he was?" said Kim.

"No," said Coutinho. "Just uphill someplace."

He turned to Hosea Hokoana, who sat on a flat rock and cradled his daughter in his arms. His face was as impassive as an Easter Island statue. Coutinho thought that was a bad sign for someone.

"Mr. Hokoana, did you get a look at the shooter?"

Hosea ignored him.

"Sir, I'm sorry for your loss, but we need your help. We need to get on this right away."

Hosea laid his daughter down and put a massive hand

against her cheek.

"I will handle this."

"It's a matter for law enforcement."

Hosea rose to his feet.

"Stop me if you can."

After the terrible price they had just paid, they had come back to a confrontation.

But then Hosea's body jerked in a spasm, and he fell hard on his side next to Jessie's body. Coutinho gaped.

Ann Wessel tugged on the taser string.

"Damn," she said, "I hated to do that."

"You'll get over it," said Coutinho. "I sure would."

"You might want to cuff him. Fast."

Coutinho saw her point. He had planned far enough ahead to bring extra-large handcuffs. He snapped them on Hosea's wrists. It would be a job to get the man on his feet and into a vehicle, but that could wait. Coutinho looked uphill where the sniper had hidden.

"Shit," said Kim. "That's going to be a tough search."

"Good thing national parks are federal jurisdiction."

Kim grimaced at the reminder of the interagency mess this was going to become. He took his cell phone from his pants pocket and flipped it open.

"Figures. No signal."

"Ann should stay here," said Coutinho. "It's her scene until the FBI gets here. You take her vehicle up to the crater and call it in."

Kim nodded. "Better get things under control."

Coutinho turned and saw what his partner meant. The worshippers were recovering their presence of mind, and they were moving toward their vehicles. Nobody wanted to stay around a situation like this. Coutinho walked toward them and held his shield up.

"Police. You'll all have to stay. You're witnesses."

"The hell with that," said a man.

"Not your choice."

No one looked impressed."

"It was one of your own people who was killed. Does that mean anything to you?"

"We'll handle it."

"Did you see something I didn't?"

The civilians looked at each other. No one said anything.

"No? I didn't think so. You don't know who did it, and you have no way to find out. We're the cops. We do."

Several people hesitated, but most continued to move.

"And I'm going to take plate numbers if you try to leave. You will talk to us sooner or later. Might as well make it now."

There was grumbling, but people started looking for places to sit and wait. Fortunately, there was no shortage of nice flat rocks.

There was nothing to provide shade, so of course the sun had to break through the clouds. Sunlight wasn't unknown on the Hilo side of the island, but Coutinho could do without it now. If he liked having his skull baked through his hair, he would have transferred to the Kona Division years ago.

He tried not to check the time too often, because impatience might infect his witnesses. Two hours later, when the first Jeeps came bearing Parks rangers, he welcomed the sight.

But the rangers milled uncertainly. Homicide investigation wasn't really their job. Another two hour passed, before two men in their thirties arrived in a Crown Victoria rented from Hertz. Even in aloha shirts they could only be FBI.

Behind them came a representative from the Hawaii County Medical Examiner and a half dozen uniformed Hawaii County police officers driving their personal vehicles with blue police cones on the roofs. Parked vehicles hugged the side of the road.

The two Feds picked Coutinho out immediately and approached.

"You made good time," he told them.

"Your chief was a big help. We appreciate the backup."

It was important to make nice, but experience had taught Coutinho that relations could start well and still deteriorate.

"Did you pinpoint the shooter's location?" said the first agent.

He had blond hair of the type than thins rapidly in early middle age. That could cost him in the subtropics.

"Things got too hot too fast. You can get a trajectory, though."

He showed the agents how the two shots had penetrated the Ford and struck Jessie. The two Feds went to the Hawaii County uniforms and organized them to search for physical evidence that the sniper might have left.

The ME crouched over Jessie's body, while several uniforms lifted Hosea to his feet. Coutinho didn't want to watch any of that too closely.

The second FBI agent spoke up. A Japanese American like him might be a local product.

"You have any idea who it was?"

"Well, let's see," said Coutinho. "The full time population of the island is about a hundred and eighty thousand. Plus ten or twenty thousand visitors at any one time. That's our suspect pool."

It was a mistake to show outsiders his frustration, but at the moment he couldn't restrain himself.

26

IT WAS COMPLICATED, and in the most annoying way. The FBI had jurisdiction over a felony committed in a national park, but the Internal Affairs divisions of the Honolulu and Hawaii County police departments wanted in. They needed to know how much damage Jessie Hokoana's unprofessional behavior had done.

That left Coutinho and his partner out of it. At the moment all he could feel was relief, but he knew the resentment would come.

He had been neglecting other cases, and he tried to feel grateful for the opportunity to sit in his office and catch up on reports.

Someone rapped knuckles on the doorframe. Coutinho looked up. Detective Phillips stayed in the hall, because there wasn't room for him in the converted closet.

"Wally Watase," said Phillips.

After everything else, it took Coutinho a moment to

remember Wally and his confession to the prostitute attacks.

"What's up?"

"He's been toughing it out, not saying a word," said Phillips. "Until about three minutes ago, that is. Now he wants to talk."

"Okay."

"I should have said he wants to talk to you. Nobody else."

"What's that about?" said Coutinho.

"Guess you'll have to ask him."

But in the hall the two FBI agents intercepted them. Phillips recognized the look of grim Federal purpose on the two men and held his hands up in a placating gesture.

"When you can spare the time, Detective."

The two feds looked frustrated

"Mr. Hokoana is a tough nut to crack," said the blond agent. "Care to show us how it's done?"

The agent produced an effortful smile in an attempt at self-deprecation. Coutinho had to give him credit.

"Can't promise anything," he said, "but I'll give it a try."

Hosea waited for them in Interview Two. He waited the way a volcano waited. Everyone hoped he would stay dormant, but the smart money planned for an eruption.

The two FBI agents took positions against the wall. Their matching poses told the story. They had already invested time in giving Hosea the silent intimidation treatment, with nothing to show for it. They had also banished Kim to the video monitor. Not for the first time Coutinho thanked the gods of his ancestors, assuming they were out there somewhere, for giving him a partner who didn't need everything explained to him. Coutinho wouldn't have to mend fences with Kim.

He took the seat across from Hosea.

"You understand we have to talk about this."

"You have to talk. I don't."

"You know time is important. We have to question witnesses, even when they're hurting. The longer it takes us to find a direction, the harder things will be."

"Then it's a good thing I don't have the same limitations as the police."

"Do you have any idea who did it?"

Hosea said nothing.

"I think you have an idea. Why would you protect him?"

"I'm not protecting anyone."

Coutinho wheedled and threatened, but it had as much effect as prodding a mountain with an ice pick. After an hour of it, he decreed a break. Hosea didn't look tired, but Coutinho was. He ignored the obvious displeasure on the faces of the two Feds, while he thought about what to do next and tried to avoid looking indecisive in front of Hosea.

Then a name appeared on his mental radar.

"Teddy Dias," said Coutinho.

The name came from the last interrogation he had conducted in this room. Jessie's fake john, Gabriel Kekili, had worked for Teddy Dias.

.Hosea gave him a stony look. It wasn't much, but it was more of a reaction than anything else Coutinho had seen.

"Forget the silent treatment, Hosea. That's not going to work. Teddy's from Oahu. Jessie did some undercover work for Honolulu P.D., which you obviously know about. We think you know Dias, or you know about him."

Hosea shrugged, but he wasn't denying it. For the moment Coutinho would settle for that.

"You know him, and you think he did the shooting. Why?"

Nothing.

"What did Jessie tell you?"

Hosea ignored him.

"Or maybe you knew about him even before you connected with Jessie again. That's it, isn't it?"

Coutinho looked at the huge man and had an idea.

"You've been away a long time. Did you meet Teddy Dias someplace else?"

Nothing.

"Was Jessie there too?"

That opened up a whole new line of thought. He would have to check with Honolulu. Maybe he would have to bluff them into thinking he already knew the story, whatever it turned out to be.

Coutinho pondered a flanking attack, and the obvious answer came to him.

"I don't have children, but it seems to me, I wouldn't just show up after twenty years and expect a big welcome."

"We're different," said Hosea.

"Who's different?"

Hokoana already seemed to regret his weakness in speaking.

"Hawaiians?" said Coutinho.

"*Ohana* is everything. Time, distance, don't change anything."

"I don't know whether I buy that. I've lived here all my life. I know all about *ohana*. So where have you been all this time?"

"Mexico."

"You just picked up and went to Mexico? What's there?"

"It's far away. That was what I needed at the time. Jessie understood."

"Did she? What kind of story did you spin for her? We checked you out, you know. You have no paper trail at all. How does anybody manage that these days?"

"People here live off the grid all the time."

"But you weren't here, Hosea."

"I was doing what I know how to do."

"Enforcement? Collections?"

"Some. Mostly I was in the underground fight game."

"Cage fights?"

Coutinho studied the massive man some more.

"I've seen guys who are into that. You don't look like them. Especially not if you've been at it for twenty years."

"I guess I'm better than them."

"But you're back. Why?"

"The reasons I had to leave don't apply anymore."

"No more Satan's Right Hand."

Hosea smiled slightly.

"What else, Hosea? That can't be all."

"Because I wasn't welcome in Mexico anymore. And I'm a father."

Hosea paused.

"Was."

"Jessie was there recently?"

"How come a cop doesn't know?"

Coutinho took that as a yes. It gave him something to work with, and a place to go next.

27

KIM WAS GIVING the windows of their rented Ford Focus a workout. He saw Coutinho noticing and grinned sheepishly.

"I've never been here."

"What, the North Shore?"

"Oahu, period."

Coutinho just nodded. In Hawaii there was nothing new about someone who had never been off the island he was born on.

Some people stayed put, while others island-hopped all the time. Some lived on one island and commuted to another every day. That could become tiresome, which he had reason to know too well.

"My ex lives in Honolulu now," he told Kim. "It's easier on her. She hated flying every day."

"She works at the crime lab, right?"

"Yeah, she's a DNA specialist."

Coutinho listened to his own tone and realized that he

still mentioned Lucy's skills with pride. That was a little weird.

"They tell me," Kim said, "that she's dating a Honolulu detective."

The question in Kim's tone said it all. He hoped it wasn't news to Coutinho.

"One of the guys we're going to meet," said Coutinho. "As a matter of fact."

Kim said nothing.

"I'm okay with that," said Coutinho.

He wondered whether anyone in the car was fooled.

"So this is Schofield," said Kim. "Been hearing about it since I was a kid. A lot of the casualties at Pearl Harbor left here in the morning and never came back."

It was a familiar story, but a safe topic.

Soon they reached the edge of the rain shadow, the narrow zone between the wet and dry sides of the island. A little farther on, precipitation would become rare, the vegetation brown and tough and the sunlight harsher. It meant they were close to their destination. A few turns later Coutinho pulled into the parking lot of the Wahiawe station.

The desk officer didn't make them wait. It might be policy, or it might be gallantry on the part of Lieutenant Ronald Tedeschi.

Coutinho had never met his successor in Lucy's affections, but somehow he recognized the man coming to meet him and Kim. It felt strange shaking a hand that presumably touched his ex-wife in intimate ways. Tedeschi was sun-bleached to the same combination of colors as Hilly Noh.

"Detectives, welcome."

Tedeschi turned and began leading them deeper into the station building.

"Captain Hideki sends his regrets. He was summoned to

Beretania Street."

Lucy would also be there at H.P.D. headquarters, which housed the crime lab.

Tedeschi opened the door of an office. Inside, another man rose from his seat at the no-frills steel table to greet the visitors.

"Jack Ferreira."

The man looked like Coutinho's cousin. He might be a relative, since both men were obviously descendants of nine-teenth-century immigrants from the Madeira Islands or the Azores.

"We would like to offer our condolences," said Coutinho.

He didn't know how much more to say. Jessie Hokoana hadn't died in the line of duty. She hadn't been behaving much like a police officer at all.

"Thanks, Detective," said Ferreira.

"Her mother has been notified?"

"We handled that earlier today. Not fun, even if she made it pretty easy for us. Not much reaction at all."

"I hate to rush things," said Tedeschi, "but we have to meet with the feds pretty soon. We should talk to them first, but..."

Coutinho knew how to translate: local cops stick together. He hoped that their solidarity wouldn't break down under the stress of this discussion.

"Okay. Jessie Hokoana."

"She did some work for us. Undercover is hard on the officer. Not everybody bounces back from it."

"You supervised her?"

"I did. I probably don't have to tell you, sometimes super-vision can't be as tight as we would wish. Bad guys tend to notice if there's a senior officer hovering."

"We think Hokoana's undercover assignment might have

had something to do with her death."

Ferreira nodded but didn't commit himself.

"What can you tell us about it?"

"It's tricky," said Ferreira. "The Dias case is still open. The prosecutor hasn't decided about trying again. And the internal affairs aspect is still open."

"It's moot now, isn't it?"

"She made cases against a lot of guys. If there was misconduct, it could be a big setback."

"If the top guy is smart," said Kim, "it's hard to get to him. How did she manage to get next to Dias?"

Rolling up a drug ring was usually a matter of starting at the bottom and leveraging each bust to the next level up.

Ferreira shrugged. "You've seen her."

"She got personally involved with Dias?"

"Yeah."

Ferreira hesitated.

"The defense attorney got some damaging admissions out of her. Juries hate entrapment, and she made us look like manipulators. And there was a factor we never thought of, this other woman. The damn judge threw a lot of evidence out. Like Dias was a choir boy until two scheming females put the idea of dealing drugs in his head."

"What other woman?"

"Chuey Almodovar's girlfriend. Delilah Iwasaki."

"Chuey Almodovar?"

"Nephew of Pedro Azucar. Major player in Mexican *pakalolo*."

"Where's this Delilah now?"

"Don't know. Probably still in Mexico."

"What kind of relationship was there between her and Jessie?"

"Looked innocent to us. Two hometown girls away from

home. Stands to reason they'd hang together. But the defense made it look sinister."

"I'm starting to understand why this assignment was so hard on Jessie. She had no support, did she?"

Tedeschi and Ferreira exchanged meaningful looks and decided that Tedeschi would do the answering.

"Like I said, we had to give her a lot of space."

"She didn't have the experience to handle it. We know she was diverted even before attending the academy."

"She knew enough to shake the Feds off her tail."

"So she was smart," said Coutinho.

As an attempt to mend fences, his remark fell flat.

"You know as well as we do," said Tedeschi, "an undercover has one big case in her. Then she's burned, and usually burned out."

"Okay, you cleaned the file you gave us on her."

"I told you, that lawyer Dias hired was smart. From your neck of the woods, by the way."

"Shit," said Coutinho. "I should have known. Agnes Fucking Rodrigues. She always turns up when I don't need her."

"Sounds like you lost a few rounds to her."

Coutinho didn't plan to rise to that provocation.

"So Hokoana was done," said Coutinho. "And yet you recommended her for our job."

The temperature in the room dropped again.

"We did," said Tedeschi. "Some of us still think she was a good cop. Like I said, an undercover can pay a serious price. She needed a change of scene, to clear her head. We also needed to keep her out of harm's way. We expected Dias to take it very personally. Disciplining her would have been a signal to his lawyer to go for the kill. We weren't about to tip them off."

"Okay."

"We couldn't put her in uniform, because that would have left her dangling where Dias could find her anytime. We figured the best idea would be to send her someplace else with a new cover story and a low-key assignment. It should have kept her away from him, and it should have kept her record clean for when she testified."

If posing as serial killer bait qualified as low-key, that said a lot about Hokoana's previous assignment.

"But it didn't," said Coutinho. He held up his hands in a placating gesture. "What we care about now is, where's Dias?"

28

THIS TIME HILLY NOH was even less pleased to see Coutinho. She was getting ready for the lunch rush, and she wanted none of whatever he was selling.

He looked at her for signs of grief, but he knew that some people just don't show it.

"Can this wait, Detective?"

"We're sorry, but it can't."

"What is it?"

"Can we sit down, please, Ms. Noh."

She didn't move. Coutinho decided to proceed.

"We're sorry for your loss."

She blinked. Coutinho began to wonder whether she had heard or understood.

But then Hilly Noh looked exhausted. She took two steps to her right and dropped into a plastic chair at a table for four in the middle of the room. Coutinho took the seat across from her. Kim pulled the chair next to Coutinho.

Hilly stared at the table top, but she probably wasn't seeing it. Her eyes stayed dry.

"I didn't really take much in earlier, when they told me. Where did this happen again?"

"Chain of Craters Road."

"What happened? It must have been cop stuff."

Coutinho had been wondering just how to handle this. It hadn't really been cop stuff. In fact, Jessie had died as a result of unprofessional behavior. But if he took the long view, her police work had stressed her beyond her breaking point.

"She was shot by a sniper."

"Do you know who?"

"Not yet."

"Did Hosea have anything to do with it?"

"Do you mean, did he kill her?"

It would be interesting if she thought that.

"He wouldn't. But trouble always followed him around. If he didn't find any, he made some."

Coutinho waited for more, but she was done with Hosea for the moment.

"Did you ever hear the name Teddy Dias?"

"No," she said after a pause. "Who's that?"

"Someone from Jessie's job."

"She met a lot of bad people."

Coutinho studied her. He had seen many people after they had received this kind of news. Hilly was shaping up as one of those who needed to stay in harness to keep herself together. He didn't plan to suggest that she go home.

He stood, and Kim followed his lead.

"Again, we're sorry for you loss."

Outside, he and Kim paused before getting back in the car.

"She knows something," said Kim. "Something to do with Dias."

Coutinho nodded.

"It's not a bad guess that Dias was one of the bad guys. But I got a bad feeling from that hesitation thing she did."

"*Tita* like her isn't going to give it up unless we get some leverage," said Kim.

Tita. A tough chick. Hilly Noh seemed to qualify.

29

"SEE, AGNES, IT'S LIKE THIS."

"You can call me Counselor, Detective."

Agnes Rodrigues always took the bait, which was why Coutinho always called her by her first name. It was one of the few ways he knew to get to her.

Her office was on Punahele, near the jail. Coutinho didn't think it looked like a woman's office. It resembled his, with no personalized touches at all. Her steel desk must have come from a government surplus auction, and someone had smuggled her two wooden client chairs out of a high school storage room. Her clients wouldn't feel comfortable in an upscale setting, but he thought she was also making a statement about her ability to play with the boys.

"But we're old friends, you and me."

"Dream on," she said.

Rodrigues was breathtaking, as always. Her business suits, rare on the island, always fit perfectly, and they always showed off her world-class legs. The rest of her was all sleek dark Portuguese beauty. His mother would be delighted if he brought someone like Rodrigues to Christmas dinner, but if he ever caught himself thinking along those lines, he would eat his gun.

"We need to talk to your client Teddy Dias. He had motive, means and opportunity to kill a police officer."

Coutinho didn't know about the means, but it was no great leap to imagine Dias with access to a rifle.

"You would be talking about Jessie Hokoana," said Rodrigues. "My client has no motive. That case was already dead."

"His record doesn't suggest that letting bygones be bygones is part of his skill set."

"Last I checked, this is the United States of America. We don't do preventive detention here. He's free to go where he wants."

"And we're entitled to talk to him."

"So do it."

"We can't find him. We're looking, but the harder we have to look, the less you want us to be the ones to find him. You've never represented a cop killer before, but I still think you know what I'm talking about."

"Alleged cop killer."

"That's not worth arguing. You know it's better if he finds us than the other way around."

"Thank you for confirming that the Hawaii County Police are out of control."

He smiled.

"No, just human. Even you should understand that."

He stood.

"Nice seeing you, Agnes."

30

COUTINHO HAD JUST PARKED at Kapiolani Street when his cell phone rang. He raised his eyebrows when he saw the number. He hadn't expected anything.

"My client has nothing to hide," said Agnes Rodrigues. "He's waiting for you at this address."

She named a street on the wetter, slightly less expensive side of Waimea.

"Thanks, Counselor. It's the right thing to do."

"I don't need your help determining what I should do."

She hung up. Coutinho looked at the address again and got a feeling. Since he was already at the station, he went to his office. He googled the address, and there it was. But what did it mean? What was Teddy Dias doing there, of all places?

As he and Kim drove north on 19, he fell into one of those strange mental states that sometimes seized him. Highway 19 was the only main artery on this part of the island, but he seemed to be seeing it for the first time. The order of the towns and beaches and state parks hadn't changed, but he examined each one in passing.

Laupahoehoe, Honoka'a. Then ranch country again.

Hilly Noh's home was a piece of old Hawaii. Even on the less developed Big Island such places were becoming rare without big money to preserve them. Current prices suggested that she had acquired the place twenty or thirty years earlier. Even if her business was doing well, the property would be beyond her means today.

A few incurious beef cattle munched grass in a fenced-in pasture adjacent to her property. Beyond the enclosure, the land swept up rapidly and became a mountain slope. The whole picture made Coutinho think that God must have had a lot of the color green left over from creating the rest of the universe and decided to use it up here.

The house was a standard small white box with window slats that cranked open and shut. A plastic roof shielded the otherwise open car port.

Coutinho drove slowly up the long driveway. Ahead of him were two black SUV's carrying large men from the Special Response Team. Kim sat beside him looking tense and not at all pleased. Gravel under their wheels announced their approach. Teddy Dias was expecting them, but for what? He could be planning a grand exit involving a shootout and as many dead cops as he could take with him.

A look out any window would tell Dias that resistance was guaranteed to be futile as well as fatal. The two SUV's stopped. Two teams of four armed and armored officers hustled out of each vehicle to surround the premises. Coutinho parked in the shelter of one of the larger vehicles.

He and Kim climbed out. Both drew their guns. The front door of the house opened, and Hilly Noh appeared. Her hands were visible and empty. The detectives stopped.

"You won't need those," said Hilly. She pointed vaguely but Coutinho knew she meant their guns.

"Is Teddy Dias there?"

"Yes."

"Where is he?"

Hilly said nothing. Coutinho turned and signaled the SRT team to join him. As the officers reached Hilly, she stepped back into the house but held the door for them. They split up and cleared the house room by room. Coutinho stayed with Hilly and watched her.

"In here," Kim called.

Coutinho took Hilly's elbow and steered her in the direction of his partner's voice. Kim was in the main bedroom. Coutinho noted a double bed, a bureau with a mirror over it, two night tables, and a trunk at the foot of the bed. There was also a large closet that would need to be searched, with two wooden sliding doors.

On the bed was a sight that made him stop and plant his feet. No matter how many times Coutinho encountered death, it still shocked him with its otherness. Life was life. Death wasn't.

He knew Teddy Dias only from mug shots. Now he would never have the pleasure of interrogating the young man. Dias was lying in a puddle of blood, and his chest was a mess. Coutinho turned to Hilly Noh, who stood between two SRT's.

"Where's the gun?"

She said nothing, but she looked toward the farthest corner of the room. Coutinho walked past the bed and looked in the two feet of clearance between the bed and the wall. A huge revolver rested on the bare wood floor. It was a near-antique that Coutinho didn't recognize. There would be time to identify it.

"What happened, Hilly?"

"He killed my daughter. And he didn't even care that I knew."

"Did he say he had killed her?"

"Not in so many words."

"What did he say?"

"He said we're both liars, but liars don't always get away with it."

"Anything else?"

"He said it was a good thing our *ohana* wouldn't continue, because lying is genetic."

"What else?"

"That was enough for me."

Teddy Dias hadn't really confessed to anything, Coutinho realized. His words could even be a denial.

"Where did the gun come from?"

"My father had it."

Coutinho nodded to Kim, who handcuffed Hilly Noh and Mirandized her. The SRT team took her away, looking like overkill with one middle-aged woman between them.

"Should have seen this coming," Coutinho said.

"How could we?"

"She's a man's woman who didn't seem to have a man around."

"Maybe Teddy hung around her to find Jessie."

That might have been part of it, but Coutinho had known other men who got a charge out of nailing two generations of women in the same line.

"Could be."

He grimaced.

"This case is still open. We need to trace his movements, see if we can place him down on Chain of Craters Road."

31

"**MY TWO FAVORITE DETECTIVES,**" said Tanaka. "I was hoping there was some way to fuck things up even worse, but I didn't think it could be done. Thank you so much for proving me wrong."

Coutinho and Kim stood in front of the Lieutenant's desk. They didn't expect him to offer them seats.

"What else can you do to ruin my day?"

Coutinho knew enough to keep his mouth shut. Tanaka continued to glare at him, but when that didn't seem to make him feel better, he waved the detectives out of the room.

"Hey, Coutinho."

Coutinho turned. It was Detective Phillips coming toward him.

"You the one put a flag on…" he consulted the printout in his hand. "…Delilah Iwasake?"

"Yeah, why?"

"She flew into Honolulu a week ago, spent a couple of

days there. Then to Kona. She's been on the island for three days."

Coutinho stared at Phillips without seeing him. The flag had been a routine precaution, but here was Chuey Almodovar's girlfriend on the island with plenty of time to involve herself in Jessie's death, and Teddy's.

That would mean Rodrigues's defense during Teddy's trial might not be just smoke blown at the jury. Could there have been some kind of conspiracy between Jessie and Delilah Iwasake that had gone bad? It wouldn't kill Coutinho to admit that Agnes Rodrigues could be right.

Would it?

"Where's this been all this time? Would have been good to know."

"Clerk didn't know what to do with it, so she gave it to me. Then I saw Dias on it and connected it to the hooker case."

Delays happened. There was no point in getting worked up about it.

The next step was to find Iwasake. It shouldn't be hard. She had booked a rental car through Hawaiian Airlines. She wasn't exactly covering her tracks. Okay, nobody actually wanted her for anything, but it was still a little disconcerting to see her acting innocent.

Coutinho went to his office and logged into his computer. He tapped out the BOLO and hit Send.

Then he started calling hotels, starting on the Kona side. It would take a while, but it would also keep him out of Tanaka's way.

But it was the BOLO that got results, and in close to record time. He had barely started on the hotels when the email popped up. A uniform had just spotted Iwasake's Nissan Versa at the Hilo Hawaiian, practically down the street.

Now Coutinho was starting to think someone was setting him up. It was probably just paranoia, but still. He looked up at Kim at his desk.

"Chuey Almodovar's girlfriend is at the Hilo Hawaiian. Let's go talk to her."

"Should we bring the SRT's?"

So Kim was also feeling a step behind.

"It's going to be a while before I bother them again."

"Just kidding. Let's go."

Even in traffic the trip took just ten minutes. The parking lot was as crowded as ever. Coutinho had to go around to the overflow lot next to the Japanese gardens near the hotel. He and Kim walked along the curved driveway and entered the lobby.

Dayton Hideki was behind the reception desk. That was good. Coutinho knew him from high school.

"Howzit, Errol?"

Coutinho introduced his partner.

"We need to talk to a couple of your guests. Nothing heavy. Just talk."

"Who?"

"Chuey Almodovar and Delilah Iwasake."

"Three-oh-four. She's there alone. I just saw him leave."

Talking to the girlfriend alone was just what he wanted, but getting it so easily made him feel that he was building up a huge karmic debt.

He and Kim turned and went to the elevators. They didn't speak during the short ascent. The hall was empty as Coutinho knocked on 304.

"Who is it?" said a female voice.

"Police, Ms. Iwasake. We'd like to speak with you."

The door opened promptly. The woman wasn't planning to play games with them. Both detectives held their shields ready.

The woman looked as Japanese as her last name. That didn't always happen in Hawaii, where the ethnic melting pot often shuffled genes. She was thirty-ish, and her lean physique showed under her black T-shirt and white pants. She had removed her shoes, Japanese-style.

"Come in."

Nothing in her tone said she was intimidated or even puzzled.

"I'm going to make a call," she said.

Coutinho started to tell her that he would set the rules, but she stopped him with a gesture.

"That's non-negotiable. It's the only way I will say a word. And we need to make this quick, before Chuey gets back."

Coutinho began to get a bad feeling.

"Go ahead," he said.

Iwasake took a cell phone from the night table and speed dialed.

"I have a situation," she told someone. "Yes, Hawaii County."

She ended the call.

"We'll have to wait a bit."

She knew how to wait, and that already told Coutinho what he needed to know. Ten minutes later his cell phone rang, and he knew who it was.

"Meet me at Ken's," said Tanaka. "Fifteen minutes."

"Do we bring her with us?"

"No. Just you."

Tanaka ended the call.

"I don't mean to be rude," said Iwasake, "but I need you to go."

Coutinho nodded. He and Kim headed for the door without another word.

In the lobby a young man in a hurry brushed by them on

his way to the elevators. They let him pass.

"That would be Chuey," said Kim.

"I guess it would."

In Ken's Coutinho scanned the dining room. Lieutenant Tanaka shared a booth with a middle-aged man of the type whose own wife can't remember what he looks like.

"Detective Coutinho, Detective Kim, meet Agent Robertson of the Department of Public Safety."

Coutinho reached down to shake the man's hand and slid in beside him. Kim sat next to Tanaka.

"Division of Narcotics Enforcement," said Robertson.

"Oh. I didn't think you guys were real."

Coutinho felt stupid for blurting the truth. Buried in the state Department of Public Safety, the Division didn't attract much attention. The rest of the Department handled corrections and security in airports and state buildings.

Robertson didn't take offense.

"We get that a lot."

"What can I do for you?"

"That's easy. You can stop looking for Delilah Iwasake."

"We found her, but I have a feeling we're going to leave it at that."

"She's one of ours," said Robertson. "Undercover."

Coutinho thought about it. His reaction was complicated but it didn't involve surprise. Overlapping layers of mutually oblivious undercover operations happened, and he should have expected it in a screw-up as total as the Jessie Hokoana case.

"I definitely didn't think you did undercover operations."

"We kind of backed into this one."

"How'd that work?"

"She met him in a bar on her own time. She wasn't interested, gave him a phony name—Delilah. He couldn't take a hint, just kept talking. Then he let it slip what he was up to. It just fell into place."

Robertson paused.

"From what we understand, that's exactly how Officer Hokoana got to Mexico. Backed her way into it."

"So you're leaving your agent in? Teddy Dias is dead. I assume he was the original target."

"He was. Before he died, we were ready to pull her out. The prosecutor had decided against retrying him, because that lawyer would be able to say, 'See? I was right.'"

Coutinho nodded. Agnes Rodrigues would know how to paint Teddy Dias as an innocent surrounded by sexy, manipulative female cops.

"But Chuey hasn't given up. She says he's determined to prove himself to Azucar. He wants to make the Hawaii connection work and then present it to his uncle."

Coutinho felt like working up a head of rage. He did it roughly once every ten years, and the novelty always got results. The problem was, he had no target for an outburst. Everyone here had fucked up with the purest of motives. And there was nothing a tantrum could accomplish.

"Thanks for the brief," he said instead.

32

PHILLIPS CAUGHT HIM again in the hallway.

"Wally Watase still wants to talk to you."

"I thought that was closed."

"A confession would sew it up just right, but he won't talk to me. He still says it has to be you."

Coutinho thought for a moment. It couldn't hurt to help another detective, not when he couldn't touch his own cases without screwing them up. Maybe he needed a breather.

"Okay, lead the way."

"I think you know where Interview Two is," said Phillips.

"Ask Tanaka if I can find my ass with both hands. You going to watch?"

"My case."

Coutinho opened the door to the interview room. The man behind the steel table was a familiar sight. As a uniformed officer Coutinho had brought Wally Watase in many times. It took ingenuity to get drunk and disorderly in Hilo after midnight, but Wally managed it most Saturdays.

That was before he married Alice Freitas and straightened up for more than ten years.

Coutinho took a seat across from the man, whose face told the life story of a mediocre boxer. The thickened ears and the scars around his eyes came from his young days in the ring. Then he had spent a couple of decades in the sun with the county road crew. Wally could still qualify in the welterweight division, but his callused hands belonged to a man several times his size.

"Howzit, Wally?"

"Not so good, Coutinho."

"I guess not. How'd you get yourself into this mess? I never figured you for a guy to cut up a woman."

"I ain't."

"You saying you didn't kill that girl?"

"Nope. Didn't hurt the other ones, neither."

"They caught you with the knife. It's the right knife. DNA proves it. You know about DNA?"

"I watch the TV some. And I know you got my fingerprints on the knife."

"So what are you trying to tell us now?"

"You know my Alice?"

"Sure. Old time Portugee *ohana*. Is that why you asked for me? Because I know Alice?"

"You know she got a son from before she married me. Lennie. I always try to do right by Lennie, but he ain't having none of it."

"That can be hard, Wally."

"The old story. 'You ain't my father.' Always threatening to go to his real father, who don't want nothing to do with him. Me, I'm right there. Maybe that's why I'm not good enough for him. He don't want nothing that he can have."

"Where's this going, Wally?"

But Coutinho thought he knew.

"He's been running wild. Drugs, stealing. But then he goes for the big one. He's the one cut those girls. I figure I take the weight for him, for Alice. But then I'm thinking, no. It ain't just about me and Alice and Lennie. As long as he's out there, he can do it again. I can't let that happen."

Ohana, Coutinho thought.

In Hawaii it came down to family. Fathers, mothers, sons, daughters. And would-be fathers and would-be sons. The family was supposed to be a place of refuge, but bad things could happen when it didn't work out that way. Who knew that better than a cop?

"Has Lennie been in jail recently?"

"Yeah. He did seven months for possession."

That explained the interval between killings.

Coutinho met Phillips out in the hall.

"I buy it," said the other detective. "I never could see Wally doing that."

"Me, either. Thanks, by the way."

"For what?"

"Wally just figured something out for me."

33

COUTINHO SAT ACROSS from Hilly Noh in the county lockup in Hilo. It struck him, not for the first time, how much time he spent in jail.

And every time he came, he wondered again what it was about jail that accelerated time. Hilly looked as if she hadn't seen the sun in years. Her defiance had also faded. Coutinho decided to go straight at her now, before her resistance returned.

"First time we met, you said Jessie didn't have time for family. I think you were being unfair. Am I right?"

"Teddy was right. I am a liar."

'You're the one who didn't have time for her."

"When Hosea left, I sent her to my mother. Supposedly until I got my head straight. Like that was ever going to happen."

"But you never sent for her."

"I met my second husband. He would have taken Jessie

in. I was the one who wanted to start from scratch."

"Which is why Jessie was so interested in her father."

"She didn't really have either of us. Thanks to me."

"Who's Abie's father?"

That jolted her out of her self-disgust. She looked up at him.

"My second husband. I have enough on my conscience. I'm not taking on anything I didn't earn."

"Who does Abie think is his father?"

"What kind of question is that? He knows who his father is."

"Okay, maybe I didn't put that the right way. Growing up, who did he wish it could be? Kids always build a fantasy world. I know I did. My real parents were the pirate king and queen. They left me here until it was time to come get me and have me take over the pirate kingdom."

Hilly looked defeated.

"You got over it, though."

"Abie didn't."

"He was obsessed with Hosea. Telling Abie about him was the biggest mistake I ever made, and believe me, I know how to make them. Abie wanted to be a warrior like King Kamehemeha."

She gave a bitter laugh.

"He'd need to grow a foot and get about two hundred pounds of muscle from somewhere, but he wanted to be Hosea. That's probably why he got into drug dealing in the first place. To be an outlaw like Hosea."

"Does he still feel that way?"

"Have to ask him."

"I think you know."

"Something changed his mind."

"What could Hosea do to disappoint Abie that much?"

"Hurt his pride."

Of course. Coutinho remembered Abie bound and gagged in the house in Kapoho. He put himself in Abie's place and imagined his life-long idol refusing to listen to a word. Maybe Abie had even begged to be taken along.

And while his mind was working, Coutinho realized that he knew where to find Abie Noh.

34

THE PLACE TO LOOK for Abie Noh was the scene of his humiliation. After his terrible mistake, the young man would be in a self-lacerating mood.

It was a no-brainer, which these days made Coutinho feel right at home.

Schilling's house looked exactly the way Coutinho had last seen it. Even the front door was flapping open again, but this time it looked forlorn, rather than ominous.

He found the young man sitting Japanese style on a decrepit mat in the main room. Coutinho winced. All of his cop experience told him that the way to build a rapport with Abie was to get down on his level. Like many islanders, Coutinho had grown up on the floor, but Lucy had shifted their lives onto chairs. He was out of practice and middle-aged on top of it.

But he had to try. He looked for a mat that wouldn't fall apart when he picked it up. That one in the far corner looked good. He kept an eye on Abie as he went for it.

"Let's talk, Abie."

"So you can put me in jail."

"Abie, it's too late to worry about that. It doesn't have to be me. If you want, I can get somebody else for you to talk to. Or to put the cuffs on when we have to go."

"I don't suppose it matters much."

"You were shooting at Hosea, right?"

Abie choked out such a violent sob that Coutinho reached toward his nine-millimeter in its holster. He stopped himself before Abie noticed.

"Jessie was okay. I didn't know her that good, but she was family. When she came to me for help, what was I gonna do? I said, cool. I can do that."

"Then Hosea came and took over."

"I could have helped him keep her safe. But he just brushed me off."

Coutinho wondered what to say next.

"I don't suppose I hit him?" said Abie. "I know he's alive, but did I at least wing him?"

"Yeah, you did."

Coutinho had never learned to enjoy lying to suspects, but sometimes that was what it took to keep someone cooperative.

"He's hard to kill," said Abie. "My mother said so."

Coutinho got a feeling.

"When did she say that?"

"Just the other day. She always thought he was dead. She was sure of it."

"How could she be sure?"

"I don't know," said Abie.

Coutinho could see that it wasn't the main thing on the young man's mind right now.

"You ready to go, Abie?"

"I guess."

"Just sit there for a minute. I have to pat you down and cuff you."

"I know how it goes."

Coutinho got up and waited a moment for the protests from his joints to subside.

"Okay, get up."

Abie didn't lie. He had done this before. He stood, turned, and put his hands behind his back. Coutinho did the handcuff routine and searched Abie, even though the young man's T-shirt concealed nothing, and his board shorts hung as if the pockets were empty. Coutinho took Abie's left elbow and steered him down the aisle and out of the church.

The sky was gray, as usual on this side of the island, but the deceptive subtropical glare still made him squint. That was why it took him a moment to recognize the threat. The man standing by Coutinho's car wasn't Kim, unless Kim had doubled in size. Coutinho didn't glance sideways, because he knew Abie was giving him a reproachful look.

You lied to me.

"What are you doing out, Hosea?"

"The charges were bullshit. You know that."

"Where's my partner?"

"On the ground," said Hosea Hokoana. "Other side of the car."

"Is he okay?"

"He'll have a headache, but he'll be fine. As long as you do the smart thing."

Coutinho didn't need to ask what that was.

"You can't have him, Hosea."

"Then I'll have to take him."

"The smart thing would be for you to give this up," said

Coutinho. "Even if you take him, we'll be right after you."

"I'll have time to do what I need to do. Back away."

"No."

"It's just you and me. Your partner can't help you."

Hosea raised his huge hands and showed Coutinho a Smith and Wesson nine-millimeter that must be Kim's. Kim was undoubtedly handcuffed as well as unconscious. Coutinho gave himself a mental kick. He had brought the Special Response Team for what had turned out to be the arrest of one middle-aged woman. To avoid looking stupid again, he had left himself dangling out here all alone. He took a quick inventory. His own nine wasn't much good. Hosea could take a clip to the body and keep coming. Besides the gun, Coutinho had his phone and his car keys. The keys might help, if he could buy a little time.

"There's nothing you can do here," said Hosea. "Nobody's going to hold it against you."

"I will," said Coutinho.

"Then that's your problem."

Hokoana took a step toward Abie, who backed up. Coutinho moved between the two men. Hosea swept him aside with a massive arm. The negligent gesture sent Coutinho staggering. Somehow he kept his feet under him.

Abie backed up again, but then he charged with a scream. With his hands immobilized behind him, he led with his head. Hosea was unimpressed. He straightened Abie up with a punch that traveled no more than a foot. Abie stood at attention for a moment and then melted to the ground.

Coutinho didn't waste the moment that Abie's kamikaze attack had bought. He sprinted toward the rear of his car. He willed his mind into clarity in spite of his need for speed, or he would fumble as he tried to insert the key in the trunk lock. Hosea turned and seemed to guess what Coutinho had in mind. The big man broke into a run.

The trunk lid popped, and Coutinho ducked inside it. Hokoana was almost on him, but Coutinho came out of the trunk with his shotgun. Hosea tried to knock the barrel aside with his forearm, but Coutinho ducked under the blow. He backed away in a crouch and racked the slide of the gun.

Coutinho looked for fear or even caution in Hosea's eyes, but there was nothing. If this was the big man's day to die, he was ready.

"You can't win this one, Hosea."

"What makes you think I care?"

"You have unfinished business."

"I know."

"I don't mean Jessie. I mean her mother. You owe her something. For walking out in the first place. You got for make *ho'oponopono*."

Hosea had to restore harmony. It should matter to him if he took the Hawaiian religion seriously.

"I didn't exactly walk out."

"What does that mean?"

Hosea grinned and pulled the right side of his 6XL T-shirt up. Coutinho looked at the ravages of the scar just below Hosea's rib cage. It was the kind of scar that came from an untreated bullet wound.

"That Hilly's one of a kind," said Hosea. "Never met any-body else like her."

"She shot you?"

Coutinho didn't really need to ask. That was what Hilly had been telling Abie.

"She did. She's probably thought I was dead for all these years. I almost was."

"Was it a big-ass revolver?"

"Yeah. I took the bullet out myself."

"Sounds like you have a lot of making up to do. *Ohana* calls."

"What would you know about that?"

"I'm fifth generation Big Island. I know all the names, all the way back to 1878."

Naming the ancestors was crucial in Hosea's traditional religion.

"I know who they are and where they came from. I belong here as much as you."

"It's not the same."

"We can discuss it."

Hosea's mouth twitched, and Coutinho could have sworn it was a smile.

"You're good. Okay. We'll talk. After I talk to Hilly."

"I'll make it happen. She's in jail."

"I know. She offered to post my bail."

Oh, Coutinho thought.

"You thought Teddy Dias killed Jessie. What changed your mind?"

"Something Jessie said. How we should have let Abie come with us. I humiliated him, and he came after me."

Now the huge man knew what pain was. His face didn't change, but for once Coutinho saw through the mask.

"Jessie paid my price."

Coutinho motioned toward the ground.

"Why don't you take a seat? And toss the gun away."

Hosea lowered himself to the dirt and leaned his back against the car, which seemed to tilt a little. Coutinho told himself it was just his imagination.

"I was never going to shoot you," said Hosea. "I only kill people who need killing."

"I have to do things a certain way. You understand."

Hosea tossed Kim's gun aside.

Coutinho let the shotgun go with his left hand. The barrel drooped a little. The gun was heavy for one hand. With his eyes on Hosea he stooped and picked Kim's nine up by the barrel. He laid the gun on the trunk of his car for the moment and reached cross his body for the cell phone on his belt. He speed-dialed headquarters and got things started there. Coutinho backed up to where he could see both Hosea and Kim, who was starting to stir.

Abie was still out.

Kim rolled over.

"How the hell did I get cuffed?"

"Hosea knocked you out."

"Oh. Yeah. Unhook me."

"You'll have to do it. I'm watching him."

Coutinho walked his keys over and dropped them where his partner could snag them with his fingers. He went back to keep an eye on Hosea.

"How come Hilly was going to bail you out?"

"Change of heart, I guess. Her lawyer says she doesn't even want to kill me anymore. She also knows she's not going to get bail. I don't think she even wants to fight the charges."

Hosea did the almost smile again.

"There's nobody like Hilly, but that lawyer comes close."

Coutinho left that one alone.

Almost an hour later the SRT team arrived, with an ambulance behind them. Abie was conscious, and Coutinho thought he might have to knock the young man out again to make him ride with the medics.

The SRTs had the extra-large handcuffs for Hosea, who made even tactical cops look puny. He also displaced one of them from the back seat of their SUV, which required the leftover officer to ride with Coutinho, Kim and Abie. The tactical officer's mood suffered from the humiliation.

"Relax," said Coutinho. "I'm looking a hell of a lot worse than you."

35

PHILLIPS AND A COUPLE of uniforms dragged Lennie Watase through the station to Interview One. As the two young officers wrestled Lennie into the room, Phillips his own lower back gently and grimaced.

"I know," said Coutinho. "I'm getting too old for the wrestling matches too."

"He got in a kidney shot. I should have puked on him. Serve him right. Time was, a moke like him would never have laid a glove on me."

"So where'd you find him?"

"Kukuihaele. He had this dimwit idea of going down into Waipi'o and living off the land. He was gonna hunt wild pigs."

"No hookers to cut up down there," said Coutinho.

The unearthly valley was all green and white. The green was for the lush plant life and the white for more falling water per square mile than anywhere else in Coutinho's experience.

Phillips snickered.

"I told him, Lennie, the only pigs you hunt are shrink-wrapped in Costco."

"He say anything else?"

"Nope. Didn't even care that we saved his life. He was also planning to drive his Escort down there."

Coutinho winced. The road down to the valley was so steep that only an all-wheel drive vehicle could grip the surface. Lennie's car would have fallen nearly a thousand feet.

"I meant about the murders. He didn't lawyer up?"

"Nope. We can keep talking to him."

"Let me give it a try."

"What the hell," said Phillips. "You did it with Wally. Maybe you've got the right touch with that bunch."

36

COUTINHO READ the young man his rights again.

"What's the use?" said Lennie Watase.

Coutinho studied him and saw a common island story. His ancestry was Portuguese at a glance, but his name said nothing about that. Lennie had a first name that anyone could have, and a Japanese surname. In Montana Coutinho had met militant advocates of racial purity, and he enjoyed making them crazy with examples from Hawaii.

"So, Lennie," said Coutinho. "What is it about hookers? You can't just rip them off for the day's receipts and let them go?"

"They piss me off."

"Do they piss you off, or are they just handy when you decide you're pissed off?"

"What's the difference?"

He had a point. For the women the result was the same.

"Was there anybody you just robbed without cutting her up?"

"I don't think so."

"Come on, Lennie. I would remember if I was you."

"You're not me."

"Okay, then we have to go through them. Nail down the details. Let's start with Gladys Robles."

"I didn't exactly get names"

"Her."

Coutinho had mug shots of the women, who all had multiple arrests. He spun a photo on the desk and slid it toward Lennie.

'Yeah, okay."

Coutinho led him through times, places, number of stab wounds. Everything hung together well enough to make a case. No one expected Lennie to remember exactly how many times he had plunged a knife into each female body.

It struck Coutinho that the women didn't resemble each other. There was no obvious common factor, except that they were vulnerable as only prostitutes are. Lennie wasn't killing a particular woman over and over.

As he worked, Coutinho began to feel better. He had the moves, no matter what his lieutenant was thinking. And that was good, because he still had Hilly Noh to deal with. He also knew Lennie's mother well enough that he owed her an informal visit. He wasn't looking forward to that.

"Okay, Lennie, that'll do it. We made a good start here."

It was more or less what he always told suspects, and it often struck him how grateful many of them were for the praise, as if he and they were colleagues.

Maybe they were. Without them, he would be out of a job.

37

"COME ON, AGNES, GIVE ME A BREAK HERE."

Hosea was right about Rodrigues. Without skipping a beat she had gone from representing Teddy Dias to defending his killer. Coutinho shouldn't have been surprised. This kind of thing happened when the criminal bar was as small as on this island.

The lawyer gave him a malevolent smile.

"Am I your worst nightmare come true, Detective? What a lovely compliment."

Rodrigues was seated next to her client in the jailhouse interview room. The steel table hid her from the waist down, which relieved Coutinho of the temptation to peek at those legs.

"You're more like a headache, Counselor."

He had almost called her a hemorrhoid, but crudity would tell her she was getting to him.

Hilly Noh didn't seem to be enjoying the repartee at all.

"We will be moving to exclude my client's statements at her home, and the gun."

"She gave us permission to enter and search."

"What was a lone woman supposed to do when she's threatened by heavily armed paramilitary forces?"

"Give it a rest, Counselor," said Coutinho. "Ms. Noh, do you have anything to say?"

"No, she doesn't."

Coutinho made a point of ignoring the lawyer and looking expectantly at the client. Hilly said nothing, which pleased her lawyer for the moment but also left Coutinho free to ask more questions.

"I think you weren't telling us the truth when you said you didn't know where Jessie was. Am I correct?"

"Don't answer," said Rodrigues.

"Yes," said Hilly Noh. "I knew she was in Hilo. She called me. She told me she shouldn't call while she was undercover, but she did."

"Why did she call?"

"To warn me that Teddy Dias might come asking about her."

"But you told him."

"Bad choices must be genetic," said Hilly. "I sure know how to make them."

Rodrigues looked ready to attack Coutinho with her long red fingernails. She must know what was coming. Instead of clawing him, she laid a restraining hand on her client's forearm.

"You are not going to blackmail my client into pleading guilty."

Hilly pulled her hand away from Rodrigues.

"It's not blackmail if I choose to plead guilty."

"Hilly," said Rodrigues, "you can't protect Jessie now. She's beyond that."

Hilly ignored her.

"It's up to you," he told Hilly. "Is that how you met Teddy Dias?"

"Jessie was right. He did come looking for her. He knocked on my door and introduced himself."

"How did he get you to tell him where she was?"

"Pillow talk."

In spite of all his experience, Coutinho was shocked. Hilly saw it on his face and gave him a smile of triumphant self-loathing.

"He said he was Jessie's boyfriend, and he was worried about her. I made coffee, we talked, and then we went to bed."

Beside her Rodrigues made a gesture of surrender that Coutinho had never expected to see from her.

"Mother of the year, right?" said Hilly. "Well, it was such a bad idea, I couldn't resist. I never could when it came to men."

"What about Abie's father? He sounds like a good man."

"He was. Ask all the guys I cheated on him with. Sometimes I think I married him to have a good man to cheat on."

"Did you cheat on Hosea?"

"I'm alive. What does that tell you?"

"It tells me you're a good shot. I saw Hosea's scar."

"He's a big target."

"Why did you shoot him, by the way?"

"He said he was leaving me."

"Didn't he explain why? Satan's Right Hand was no joke."

"I think that's the problem with being Hosea. He never had to explain anything to anybody, and he never learned how. Of course, I might have shot him anyway."

This was interesting but not really part of the case. Coutinho told himself to get back to business.

"Okay, you were making pillow talk with Teddy Dias, and you let it slip that Jessie was in Hilo."

"He said he wanted to tell her there were no hard feelings."

"And you bought that line?"

"Well, he was cute."

"Did he tell you what happened in Mexico?"

"I wasn't really interested."

Hilly shrugged. Coutinho grimaced. Everyone who could tell him what happened in Mexico was dead, a fugitive, or undercover.

Except Hosea, and he wasn't the sharing type.

"But then he stopped being cute," said Coutinho.

"When I thought he killed Jessie. I figured it was finally time for me to be a mother. So of course I fucked it up."

"Did he see it coming?"

Coutinho thought he knew the answer to that one. From Teddy's position on the bed, he probably hadn't even twitched.

"Men are clueless."

"Really."

"You, for instance. You have no idea that my lawyer is hot for you. You could wrap her around your finger if you wanted to."

Coutinho froze. He wouldn't have looked at Rodrigues to save his life. Or hers.

"Relax," said Hilly. "She'll never do anything about it."

Coutinho tensed as he waited for Rodrigues to take the offensive to prove her client wrong.

But nothing came.

Never in Coutinho's experience as a detective had a suspect ever seized control of an interview so completely. It was a good thing that Hilly Noh wasn't interested in beating the rap.

He wondered whether he should turn the case over to Kim, or another detective who could start from scratch.

But to do that he would have to get out of this room, and how was he supposed to do that?

"I think we're done here," said Rodrigues. "You got what you want."

At first Coutinho couldn't imagine what she meant, but then he remembered that he had just secured a confession.

38

"AMAZING," COUTINHO SAID to no one in particular.

Kim glanced at him and waited for an explanation.

"Even Agnes can surprise me once in a while."

Kim knew what he meant.

"Letting her client talk to Hosea. We could be listening in for all she knows."

"I told her we wouldn't, and she just nodded. I hope she doesn't have terminal cancer or something."

"You do?"

"I'd miss fighting with her."

"If you start dating her, it's over between us."

"Don't worry about that."

The banter was getting a little desperate. Coutinho felt relieved when Hosea appeared on the monitor. He took up the whole screen. The big man sat across the steel table from his ex-wife.

Coutinho wouldn't listen, but Rodrigues understood he

had to watch and make sure no one got violent.

And the violence could go either way.

On the other hand, the whole thing might be a waste of time. Together again after twenty years, the middle aged man and middle aged woman looked at each other. None of Coutinho's experience with suspects or witnesses had prepared him to read the thoughts behind their impassive facades.

Finally, Hosea lips started to move.

"Why the hell is the sound off?"

It took Coutinho a moment to realize that the voice couldn't be Hosea's.

Tanaka reached for the button on the wall. Coutinho wanted to wait for his heart rate to return to something like normal, but he didn't have time.

"We made a deal, Lieutenant."

"You did. I didn't."

"That's not going to play with Rodrigues."

"Who gives a shit?"

"Sir, we have to deal with her. Like it or not, we have to. We can't break a deal."

"This isn't privileged, and she knows it. That means we listen."

He pressed the button.

Coutinho resisted the urge to groan or close his eyes in pain. The only way to preserve bearable relations with Rodrigues would be to tell her that he had been outranked. Trying to keep the collapse of their deal a secret was not an option. Nixon, Reagan and Clinton could all have told him that it was the cover up that killed you.

For her part, Rodrigues would never admit it, but she understood how shit flowed downhill and puddled around the feet of front line cops.

Coutinho pushed those thoughts away. Hosea's voice was coming through.

Listening was no fun. Every sentence that came from Hosea or Hilly seemed to force its way through the painful pauses.

ACKNOWLEDGMENTS

To Elaine Ash and Andie Tucher, who read early drafts of this book and made crucial contributions to what it became; to the whole crew of writers at Shade Bar and KGB Bar, who sat through my early attempts to shape this material; and to Debbie and Fred Tucher for their hospitality during my many visits to Hawaii, my warmest thanks. I couldn't have done it without you all.

ALBERT TUCHER is the creator of prostitute Diana Andrews, who has appeared in more than seventy hardboiled short stories in venues including *The Best American Mystery Stories 2010*. Her first longer case, the novella *The Same Mistake Twice*, was published in 2013. Albert Tucher's favorite place on earth is the rainy side of the Big Island of Hawaii, and Diana says it's about time he started writing about it. He works as a librarian at the Newark Public Library.

A BRUTAL BUNCH OF HEARTBROKEN SAPS

BY NICK KOLAKOWSKI

1.

LISTEN.

At some point, a poor sap will look at you and say, "This is the worst day of my life."

But as long as you have breath in your lungs to say those words, you're not having your worst day. You haven't even hit rock bottom, much less started to dig. You can still come back from a car wreck, or that terrifying shadow on your lung X-ray, or finding your wife in bed with the well-hung quarterback from the local high school. Sometimes all you need to solve your supposedly world-ending problems is time and care, or some cash, or a shovel and a couple of garbage bags.

If you see me coming, on the other hand, I guarantee you're having your worst day. Not to mention your last.

Let me show you how bad it can get. How deep the hole goes. And the next time your idiot friend says something about worst days, as the two of you stand there watching his house burn down with his pets and one-of-a-kind porn collection inside, you can tell him this story. It might even shut him up.

Let me tell you about Bill, my last client.

2.

BILL AWOKE, as one sometimes does, dangling upside-down over a pit, ankles wrapped in heavy chains, sweat stinging his eyes, head throbbing like a dying tooth. He heard a dog bark in the night, and the muted roar of what he guessed was the Interstate, but the only light came from a bare yellow bulb bolted to a corrugated-metal shed far below.

Had he ever woken up in a more dangerous position? Bill racked his brain, recalling maybe five years ago when he'd opened his eyes to find both barrels of a 12-gauge shotgun staring back, the trembling weapon brandished by a cuckolded husband. (Only Bill's incredible gift for gab had gotten him out of that situation with his guts lead-free.) Or the time he dozed off behind the wheel and his car plowed into a ditch, the crunch of metal waking him up long enough for the steering wheel to whack him unconscious. He still had the scar on his chin from that one.

Even so, his current situation was a gold-medal contender for Crappiest Ever. His arms, twisted hard behind his back and bound at the wrists, tingled from lack of blood. They had secured the chain around his ankles with a jumbo padlock, hard to pick even if he had the tools, or could bend upwards enough to reach it.

He turned his head away from the bulb, letting his eyes adjust to the dark. Forty feet below, the pit bristled with huge shapes, hard angles; the faint moon glinted silver on the curve of a car windshield. If he fell down there, some piece of rusted-out machinery would turn him into a bit of raw meat on a shish-kabob.

"At least I still have my clothes on," he muttered into the breeze.

"Not for long," came a familiar voice, followed by a high-pitched squeal of laughter. The bartender. Of course. Bill shook his head like a Magic 8-Ball, hard, until memories of the recent past floated to the surface.

By Thomas Pluck

Bad Boy Boogie

By Robert J. Randisi

Upon My Soul
Souls of the Dead
Envy the Dead

By Rob Riley

Thin Blue Line

By Linda Sands

3 Women Walk
Into a Bar (TP only)
Grand Theft Cargo

By Charles Salzberg

Devil in the Hole
Swann's Last Song
Swann Dives In
Swann's Lake of Despair
Swann's Way Out

By Scott Loring Sanders

Shooting Creek and Other
Stories

By Ryan Sayles

The Subtle Art of Brutality
Warpath
Let Me Put My Stories In You (*)

By John Shepphird

The Shill
Kill the Shill
Beware the Shill

By Anthony Neil Smith

Worm (TP only)
All the Young Warriors TP only)
Once a Warrior (TP only)
Holy Death (TP only)

By Liam Sweeny

Welcome Back, Jack

By Art Taylor, editor

Murder Under the Oaks:
Bouchercon Anthology 2015

By Ian Truman

Grand Trunk and Shearer

By James Ray Tuck, editor

Mama Tried 1
Mama Tried 2 (*)

By Nathan Walpow

The Logan Triad

By Lono Waiwaiole

Wiley's Lament
Wiley's Shuffle
Wiley's Refrain
Dark Paradise
Leon's Legacy

By George Williams

Inferno and Other Stories
Zoë

By Frank Zafiro and Eric Beetner

The Backlist
The Short List

VISIT DOWNANDOUTBOOKS.COM

CPSIA information can be obtained
at www.ICGtesting.com
Printed in the USA
LVOW12s0630240517
535630LV00003B/156/P